The author wishes to thank several friends who have assisted with the accuracy of certain points in the storyline.

Contact the author via his agent: iechalmers@btinternet.com

By the same author:

Cycle touring:
Ten Tales of Two Wheeled Touring
More Tales of Two Wheeled Touring

Running:
Fun on the Run

Amateur music:
Pick 'n' Bix (Banjo and Trumpet Fun)

Children's story (7- 9 years):
Annabelle's Big Bike Adventure

Risky child and teenage behaviour in the 50's, 60's and 70's
Stayin' Alive – close shaves and scary episodes

The Acacia Close Mystery

Ian Cameron

Wednesday 12th April

Adrian was emerging from his early afternoon snooze.

He'd begun to watch the one o'clock news but after just a few minutes he'd opted to listen with his eyes closed. In no time at all, he'd dozed off, missing the main news, the regional news, and the national weather forecast.

Following his nap, and just as he was attempting to work out what time of day it was, he was brought to his senses by a shout followed by a loud metallic crash. Both sounds seemed to come from outside.

He knew it would be neighbourly if he investigated.

Adrian turned off the TV and found his shoes. He opened his front door. There was nothing untoward.

Retracing his steps, he unlocked the back door and stepped out on to his patio. There was nothing to see here either.

He'd definitely heard a noise.

Just then the doorbell rang. Adrian went back through the house and opened the front door. It was Colin from the house opposite.

"Hi, Adrian. I was in my garden when I heard a crash. I just popped over to make sure you were OK."

"Yes, all well here," Adrian replied. He was just about to ask Colin if his bin had been emptied when Colin interrupted.

"I'm wondering if Ted's OK," he said. "He was cleaning out his gutters earlier. You know, 'Tarzan of the Apes' at the top of his ladder."

"Right," said Adrian. "Maybe we should have a look round the back."

The pair set off down the flagged path between the two houses. Ted had a side gate, but he'd left it unlocked to allow the return of his bin.

As they turned the corner, Adrian jumped. “Oh, my word,” he said, which was the closest he ever got to swearing. Colin looked aghast.

There, on the concrete patio, was Ted lying awkwardly with his legs entangled around the rungs of his ladder.

Adrian squatted down and asked Ted if he was OK but received no response. His First Aid training came to the fore as he checked for a pulse and for signs of respiration. He found neither.

“Better call for an ambulance,” he said, walking swiftly back to his house.

The control operator was calm and reassuring as he checked Adrian’s full name, the post code of Ted’s property and whether the casualty was conscious. The operator said he would despatch a first responder paramedic as soon as he could.

In the meantime, Adrian returned to Ted’s patio to find that Colin had put the cushion from a nearby garden chair under Ted’s head. He’d also recovered Ted's donkey jacket which had been carelessly tossed over a wheelbarrow, and he'd placed it over Ted, in an attempt to keep him warm.

Both Adrian and Colin were surprised how quickly the paramedic arrived.

"I was in the locality," he said. "I'm Tony, the advanced paramedic. There'll be a crewed ambulance arriving just as soon as they clear at The Victoria."

Tony knelt next to Ted. "Can you hear me, Ted?" he asked several times. He attempted to take Ted's pulse but didn't comment. Blood began seeping on to the cushion from underneath Ted's head.

Tony took out his radio and asked control to send the next available ambulance. Colin and Adrian could only watch as the paramedic worked on his patient trying to provoke a response, or even signs of breathing.

The trio heard the siren of the ambulance in the distance, but the crew switched it off as they turned into the close. “Maybe you two should wait indoors,” Tony suggested.

They retreated to Adrian’s kitchen wondering what could have happened.

“I’ve told him a dozen times,” said Adrian. “Whenever he’s up that ladder, he doesn’t take enough precautions. When he’s cleaning his windows, he tries to save time by stretching rather than climbing down to move the ladder. He often has one foot on the rung and his other one sticking out at the side to balance.”

“True,” said Colin. “I was watching him cleaning out his front gutters this morning. He was using one hand to trowel the muck out and the other to hold the bucket. I’m not sure how he manages to balance with just his feet for support.”

There was a knock on the front door. It was the second paramedic. “We’re taking Ted on a blue light to the Vic. Here’s the front door key – we’ve locked up. Do you know if he had any relatives?

Can you contact them and tell them what's happened?"

Adrian nodded before rejoining Colin in the kitchen.

"Blimey, that was a turn up for the books," he muttered. They both heard the siren as the ambulance sped off.

"What'll we do now?" asked Colin. "I don't think Ted has any relatives."

"We should probably secure his house and while we're at it we can look for an address book. I'm sure he has a niece called Susan," Adrian suggested. "Lives in Kent, I think."

It didn't take them long to find a small address book next to Ted's telephone. Susan's mobile phone number was listed under Ted's surname – Watt. Adrian picked up the phone and dialled.

A female voice answered, "Hi, Uncle Ted, this is a surprise, it's not like you to ring."

"It's not your Uncle Ted," said Adrian. "I'm Adrian, his next-door neighbour. I'm afraid your uncle's had a bit of an accident. He fell off his ladder and is now in The Vic."

After exchanging contact details, Susan said she'd phone the hospital and if necessary, she'd drive up at the weekend. Adrian told her that, in the meantime, he'd keep an eye on the house.

Colin and Adrian looked at each other. "What an unexpected turn of events," said Adrian, "Fancy a brew?" They made their way back to his kitchen.

o-O-o

From her phone call to the hospital, Susan found out that her uncle had died. She telephoned Adrian to advise him. She added that she needed a few days for the news to sink in but planned to visit Acacia Close on the forthcoming Saturday to sort a few things out.

The next day, Colin went round the other five houses to tell the neighbours what had happened. Almost all were at work during the day but despite the close being normally quiet, it seemed eerily quiet immediately after everyone became aware of the incident.

Colin also managed to tell their regular postman, Paul, who said, “Thanks, but I am obliged to continue delivering any mail addressed to the house. It’s Royal Mail regulations.”

o-O-o

Adrian

Born and bred in Cheshire, Adrian Crawley had lived in the county for all of his fifty-four years. Happily married for 33 years, he was devastated when his wife, Pat, developed an aggressive form of breast cancer two years previously. Pat Crawley didn’t suffer for too long, but her death left a huge gap in Adrian’s life.

Their two children were now grown up and lived miles away in opposite directions – one in Penzance and one on the Isle of Skye. Adrian’s three bedroomed detached house was comfortable, probably too large for a single man, but useful when his kids and their young families came to stay.

Managing the garden filled in the long summer days, but he lacked a role in life. Putting away everyone's wheelie bins after the bin lorry had called was a minor responsibility, as was keeping the community notice board in the village up to date. And these days, the cryptic crossword took just a couple of hours each day to complete.

Adrian had tried the local bridge club after Colin had joked, "You could join that club if you play your cards right." But all Adrian found was a group of very serious players who spent most of the afternoon staring at the cards in their hands. There was little in the way of laughter, or even conversation.

On one occasion, he forced himself to pop along to the weekly sequence dancing session in the community hall but was put off when half a dozen partnerless women mobbed him.

It was hard being a widower and he almost missed being at work.

Adrian had started out as an engineering apprentice in a cereal packing company where he served his time to become a toolmaker. He was a member of the AUEW and later became a moderate, but active, shop steward. Later, he was invited to become the AUEW representative within the management services team. This small department conducted studies into work improvement methods and staffing levels within the plant. The role broadened over time to that of project management where he could be called upon to take on a variety of mixed and varied projects around the factory.

When he turned 50, the company was unexpectedly taken over. Production transferred to the predator's factory in Ireland. Adrian was given the opportunity to be redeployed but took a generous redundancy package instead.

He immediately set up "Adrian Crawley Associates" and had some business cards printed listing some of his services – systems audits and investigations. He contacted everyone he could think of to tell them about his availability and to his, and Pat's surprise, the work simply poured in. Adrian could work from home, and he loved the variety of assignments, usually analysing a particular work situation, or advising on workplace procedures.

When Pat took ill, Adrian wound his business down. And once Pat had passed away, he didn't have the appetite to continue.

But you never know what's around the corner.

o-O-o

The same day that Colin had advised the neighbours, (the day after Ted's fall and subsequent demise), Adrian popped over to Colin's to suggest that they do a bit of tidying up prior to Susan's arrival at the weekend. They started outside, putting Ted's donkey jacket, ladder, trowel, and bucket away in the garage.

Colin turned on the garden hose to wash down the patio and the pair used the house key to go in and commence a preliminary tidy up.

The previous day's dishes were still in the sink, but they made quick work of the washing up. Adrian rescued the post from the doormat – mainly leaflets advertising pizzas and tree pruning, in amongst the more important looking 'brown envelope' communications. They stacked the correspondence neatly on the hall table ready for Susan to vet.

The pair unplugged all the electrical appliances before closing the blinds and curtains and locking up.

o-O-o

Saturday 15th April

During Saturday afternoon, Susan arrived from Dartford, parking her white BMW on the driveway in front of her uncle's house. Adrian heard the car and went out to meet her.

"Good journey?"

"Not bad, thanks," said Susan, "You must be Adrian."

"Fancy a brew?"

“I could murder one,” she replied.

As Adrian showed Susan into his lounge, he spotted Colin and his wife, Michelle, walking across. Adrian had already tipped Colin off. He felt Colin should be involved in any discussions and suggested that Michelle should accompany him to make sure that Susan would feel at ease.

Once everyone was settled, Adrian brought in a tray of cups, saucers, milk jug, sugar basin, some paper serviettes and a teapot of tea. Oh, and a plate of Fox’s Assorted Biscuits. Pat had trained him well.

He resisted saying, “I’ll be mother,” as he served the drinks.

“Can I start by offering my condolences?” Adrian ventured.

“That’s kind,” replied Susan, “But not at all necessary. I hardly knew my uncle. You see, my dad and his brother were estranged. I vaguely remember coming here when I was a young girl, aged about 6 or 7. He was never a warm or cuddly uncle – very remote. I used to refer to him as my wicked uncle. Maybe I'd been reading too many storybooks. My dad never really spoke about him. I phoned him up when my dad died but he never bothered to attend the funeral. Sad really, how families fall out."

"Have you any brothers or sisters?" asked Colin.

"No, there's just me. I have some cousins on my mother's side. I see them from time to time. We have at least one annual meet up for a few days' break in a cottage somewhere. As for Ted's family, I think I have one or two second cousins, but we don't keep in touch. Dad and I never exchanged Christmas cards with that side of the family."

Adrian pushed the biscuits towards Susan.

"Not for me, thanks, I'm a bit of a health freak and I try to avoid sugary snacks."

"Will you be staying in a hotel or in the house tonight?" asked Michelle.

"Oh, the house. Why pay out money when there are spare beds next door," Susan replied.

"So, any plans for what you want to achieve this weekend?" asked Adrian.

"Well," said Susan, "I'll need to report my uncle's death to the local council. I'd like to identify my uncle's banks so I can freeze his accounts. I'd like to contact a funeral director too, to open discussions for when his body is released but most of all, I'd like to look through his papers to see if he left a will."

"We're here to help you, Susan," remarked Adrian. "You're still working full time, but Colin and I are retired."

"That's reassuring", said Susan, "I have already arranged some time off under the company's bereavement arrangements, but I've also had some early thoughts about asking for a 6-month sabbatical to give me time to sort out his estate."

“I don’t think we know where you work, Susan,” probed Adrian.

“Nothing special. I work in the claims department of one of the big insurance companies. It’s a desk job, examining people’s claims for insurance payouts and speaking to clients on the telephone. Some of the calls are easy but it can become a bit heated when I am refusing a claim. These days there are more and more chancers, or people who have not read their policies closely enough.”

“What are you doing about food?” asked Michelle.

“Well, if you kind folks can point me in the direction of a supermarket locally, I’ll stock up on milk, bread and a few basics.”

“How about the four of us go to the Toby Carvery this evening? It will save you cooking tonight, Susan.”

“Sounds like a plan. I haven’t really had anything since breakfast. If it’s not too far, I’d prefer to walk. I’ve been sat down all day.”

"It'll be busy on a Saturday night. Maybe we should try for an early booking," added Adrian.

"Great," said Susan, "I'd best go and unpack, change out of these scummy clothes, and have a bit of look around the house."

Adrian passed her the front door key.

At 5.30 the four met up again outside Adrian's house and commenced the half-mile walk to the pub. Normally, Adrian would have jumped in his car, but he took his lead from Susan.

Adrian had taken the precaution of requesting a quiet table.

"Can I take your drinks order?" asked a waitress whom Adrian thought looked about 12 years old.

"A pint of Stella for me, please," said Adrian. "Same here," added Colin, "and a Zinfandel wine for Michelle, please."

"Could I just have tap water, please?" asked Susan, "and, it says on the menu that any veggie dishes need to be pre-ordered. Broccoli parcel for me, please."

Susan explained that she'd decided to sleep in the back bedroom. There was a single bed which was made up, and she'd aired the sheets. Susan added that the house seemed to be what she imagined a single man's home would be like with some general clutter. "But the washing up's been done and things put away," she added.

"That was us," said Colin sheepishly. "Couldn't have you turning up at a dirty house."

As the early evening wore on, the four got to know each other a little better. Susan felt comfortable in their company and was warmed by the northern welcome she'd received.

As they walked back to Acacia Close, Adrian said, "I don't want to tread on your toes, Susan, but I'm more than happy to assist with any sorting out, or completion of paperwork. I'm just next door if you need anything."

o-O-o

Sunday 16th April

The next day was Sunday. As Adrian opened his bedroom curtains, he was astonished to see Susan running back up the close in full running kit. It was still only nine-thirty.

Adrian's normal Sunday morning routine was breakfast, followed by his Sunday Times, which he had delivered. He always started with the sports section before progressing to the main newspaper and then to the TV page. He liked to use a coloured highlighting pen to identify his anticipated weekly viewing plans. After that there were the financial, home, and travel supplements, though the last of these was of little interest since Pat had died.

Adrian was part way through checking the FTSE 100 prices when his doorbell rang. It was Susan.

"Good morning!!!" she bellowed in a sing-song voice, just like the Debbie Reynolds song from the film, 'Singin' in the Rain'.

"I just wondered if you'd like to help me make a start on my uncle's papers. And while we're at it, is there a funeral director you'd recommend?"

"I'll be right round," said Adrian.

"Wow!" thought Adrian, "this is the most motivated I've been for a long time." He put on his shoes, picked up his glasses and followed Susan next door.

"What's the plan?" asked Adrian.

"Well, maybe his study first and then we can have a think about what's next."

Adrian felt a bit awkward about going through his neighbour's things, especially as the funeral was yet to take place, but it was important to locate Ted's will and bank account details.

Ted appeared to have been very organised, and this made the pair's task a lot easier.

"I have no idea what my uncle did for a living but looking through a few files last evening, it seems like he ran his own company offering personal training services and exercise classes," said Susan.

"That's right. I had a conversation with him over the fence once. He was bragging about how his company was expanding all the time," said Adrian.

"Let's start in one corner and work our way around the room," suggested Susan.

Adrian put to one side, anything that looked like old bank statements. He was thinking it was a good job Ted had kept old fashioned paper records in Lever Arch files rather than electronic records, which he might have struggled with. It seemed that Ted had traded as, Watt and Wyatt Personal Training Services Limited. Susan had no idea who Wyatt was.

By late morning, they had made two piles of 'items of interest'. These were anything identifying a bank or building society account, and a pile with Company invoices and receipts but there was no sign of a will.

"How would we know if he'd instructed a solicitor?" asked Susan.

"Well, these latest invoices and receipts show that he was trading as a limited company. I can look up Watt and Wyatt on the Companies House website. There may have been a solicitor involved in the drawing up of the Articles of Association and, if so, he or she may be able to answer the question."

After spending a couple of hours sifting files, and conscious that Susan needed to travel south that afternoon, Adrian proposed pausing the search-cum-tidy. He would look up the Companies House website in the morning.

In the meantime, Susan would take Monday morning off as part of her compassionate leave. This would give her time to telephone the banks and building societies. And she would also complete the 'Tell us once gov.uk' online form. She'd taken Ted's address book so she could inform those she thought may wish know about her uncle's death.

As regards recommending a funeral director, Adrian struggled. He'd dealt with three different providers in recent years – for his mother's funeral, his mother-in-law's and his wife, Pat's. He was very suspicious of the so-called profession. He felt that representatives from all three had been pushy, especially when it came to suggesting the level of service he may require. He had to negotiate hard to ensure that Pat had a simple but dignified funeral.

Adrian recalled that, at the time, the funeral director was aghast at his suggestion that all they had to do was deliver Pat to the crematorium where the mourners would be gathered. Adrian had already arranged for a vicar (a friend of Pat's) and he'd ordered funeral flowers to place on Pat's coffin. He'd even prepared the orders of service on his computer and printed them off on card. In his opinion there was little left for the funeral director to do.

The funeral company seemed to be wanting to charge £2,000 for not a lot. Adrian went to a rival funeral director to see what they'd charge to simply move Pat from the chapel of rest to the crematorium. They were extremely cagey about entering discussions.

"We have to work together, you know."

Adrian had one last attempt, "Look, all I'm asking you to do is to deliver a box from one location to another. DPD would do it for forty quid!"

In the end, he bartered the first company down to £1,000 but it still felt too much for a simple transportation.

Since then, Adrian had spotted an advertisement in the local press. An out-of-town funeral director was offering simple cremations at a reasonable price. He drew Susan's attention to the advert.

o-O-o

Susan

Susan was newly 42. She had been married, briefly, in her mid-twenties but after just two years, her husband had absconded with a work colleague. It was a devastating blow. She took some comfort in giving him an ultimatum to collect his things on a given date but when he failed to appear, threw all his clothes on to the front path from an upstairs window. Susan was terribly hurt, and it took a long time for the wounds to heal.

After selling their marital home, Susan moved into a flat and gradually became used to living alone. She enjoyed playing in a weekly netball session at the local sports centre and met up with friends for coffees. Susan wasn't a big fan of dinner parties, or other social gatherings, where she was inevitably the token single person.

On reaching 35, Susan decided that she didn't want to become, in her own words, "frumpy, fat, and forty". One of her friends suggested that she joined a running club. At first, this seemed like an anathema, but she made a few google searches. Dartford Harriers looked a little too serious, but Dartford Running Club appeared more suited to beginners. She loved the friendly atmosphere. It certainly improved her confidence and her fitness.

After seven years of running, and approaching 42, Susan often reflected on what the future held. Her job had become repetitive, her mum and dad had passed away, and the proceeds of their estates had all come to her, meaning she was more or less, self-sufficient.

Like Adrian, she felt the sorting out of Uncle Ted's affairs had the makings of bringing a new purpose in her life.

o-O-o

Friday 21st April

On Friday evening, Susan drove north once more. The traffic was horrendous. She stopped part way for something to eat and to text Adrian to say she'd be arriving after eleven and not to wait up. She didn't realise that Adrian normally went to bed at half past nine.

o-O-o

Saturday 22nd April

Adrian thought he'd better get up early just in case Susan was going to repeat her "Singing in the Rain" routine. But he needn't have. At 08.30 he heard Susan driving off down the close. She didn't return until just before ten. She rang Adrian's doorbell at ten thirty.

"Just done the local parkrun," Susan beamed, "Have you heard of it?"

"Can't say I have," said Adrian.

"Ooh, it's a great way to start the weekend."

"Wouldn't do me."

"You should try it," gushed Susan, "All sorts of people do it – runners, people pushing kids in buggies, people with dogs and there are loads of walkers. It's a run rather than a race. And nobody is ever last – there's always a tail walker who chats to anyone near the back. Some people go for a coffee afterwards."

"Hmmm. You won't see me in a pair of shorts. You haven't seen my spindly legs!"

"We could do it together one Saturday if you like."

Adrian didn't know how to react. He liked the idea of having an interest, or a reason to get out of bed, but a run! He decided to say no more and quickly changed the subject to Ted's affairs.

They'd been talking in Adrian's kitchen for about twenty minutes when the doorbell rang. Adrian could see the shape of someone in a dark uniform through the glass.

"Good morning, Sir," said the police officer. "I'm Constable Liv Briers from Cheshire Police. I wonder if I could come in to ask a few questions about the recent accident to your neighbour, Mr Watt. Nothing too heavy, just a chat about what you saw."

"Might need Colin," said Adrian, "Won't be a tick."

Liv sat down in Adrian's lounge and took out her notebook. Adrian returned with Colin.

"Neither of us actually saw him fall," offered Adrian. "Earlier on, we'd both seen Ted up his ladder doing some gutter cleaning. Just after lunch, I heard a loud crash and when Colin and I went round the back, Ted was lying on the patio with his legs wrapped around his ladder."

"I'd say he'd stretched too far, overbalanced, and his ladder had slipped," Colin added.

"Well, we can't jump to conclusions," said the officer, "though the ambulance crew did report it as a fall. My job is to make further enquires before filing a report for the coroner. I'm charged with interviewing any witnesses. Unless there are suspicious circumstances, any incident like this is normally classed as an accidental death."

"Well, the only thing I would add," said Colin, "would be Ted's ill-regard for safety. He was forever climbing that ladder and hanging off at crazy angles whether cleaning his windows or cleaning out his gutters. I spotted him once teetering near the top adjusting his TV aerial. It may sound uncaring, but I'm really not surprised he fell off."

"Anything to add?", Liv asked Susan.

"Not really. I live down in Kent and haven't visited my uncle for years."

"Anyone know if he had any enemies, or people who'd want to harm him?" asked Liv.

"No idea," said Adrian. "He was one of the quieter residents in the close. He'd say, 'Good morning' and chat over the fence. He even joined in the street party for the Queen's Jubilee, well a bit. He ran his own business, but he only ever spoke about how successful it was."

Liv folded over her notebook, thanked everyone for their time, and said she would be reporting back to the coroner's office. She passed a business card to Susan. "Give me a ring if you think of anything else," she said, before leaving. On the card was a phone number and 'PC Olivia Briers'.

After Liv had left, Colin asked the others, "What do police officers put in their sandwiches?"

"Truncheon meat."

o-O-o

The three sat down again before exchanging what they'd been up to.

Susan went first.

The online notification process had gone well. Susan just needed a death certificate from the hospital to confirm she wasn't making things up.

Susan had also contacted Fletchers, a funeral company who promised natural cremations. Her discussions with them had been positive. She'd chosen a cardboard coffin and having listened to Adrian's previous diatribe, she had arranged for a simple delivery to the crematorium. She anticipated few mourners and had requested a humanist ceremony. The company said they couldn't do anything until Ted's body was released by the hospital, but they would remain in touch with the mortuary administrator.

Susan had also attempted to contact Ted's relatives and others whose names were in his contacts book, but with limited success. Most had simply said, "Thank you for letting us know."

Susan concluded that her uncle had not been hugely popular.

"Oh, and another thing. I've been granted my 6-month sabbatical," Susan beamed.

Adrian went next.

He told Susan that it had been very easy to look up details on the Companies House website. He'd put in 'Watt and Wyatt Personal Training Services Limited' and was astonished to find that it was listed as having been 'Compulsorily Liquidated' less than six months previously. He also discovered that annual accounts had not been filed for the previous three years.

Edward Watt was listed as the owner and the Company Secretary was shown as Neil Mowatt, a solicitor based in Chester. There was no one called Wyatt listed as a director.

"Curious," remarked Susan.

"That's not all. I searched for Neil Mowatt on the Solicitors Regulation Authority website. There is a

Chester based solicitor of that name practising as a sole proprietor. I wanted to wait for your visit before proceeding."

"OK," said Susan, "Let's have a quick look in Uncle Ted's address book. Aha! Here we go – Neil Mowatt with two phone numbers – a landline and a mobile. I'll phone this guy up to see if he knows anything about a will but won't mention the liquidation. If I ring him from my uncle's landline, he won't be suspicious."

Susan disappeared but returned after just a few minutes.

"Rude man!" she exclaimed. "I rang his mobile and he answered straight away. I started by telling him that my uncle had died. He didn't seem at all phased. Then I asked if he knew anything about a will. 'How should I know?' he said before adding, 'I need to go' and putting the phone down on me."

"Well," suggested Adrian, "We can have another search and if nothing is forthcoming, you can apply through the Probate Office to register yourself as the only close relative. The administration of your uncle's estate should be granted to you."

o-O-o

Monday 24th and Tuesday 25th April

During the next couple of days, and while Susan was still in temporary residence next door, the coroner's office telephoned Susan on her mobile phone. She had left her contact details when she first phoned the hospital two weeks previously. The coroner confirmed that he'd received the report from the Ambulance Service and the police plus an opinion from the A&E consultant. The coroner said that before issuing his conclusions, he wanted to ask if she had any reason to believe her uncle's death was anything other than an accident. She replied, "no," and the coroner confirmed that it would be recorded as an accidental death caused by an injury to the head following a fall. He said a death certificate would be issued to her shortly.

The death certificate arrived two days later. Adrian assisted Susan in commencing completion of the forms for the Probate Office.

Susan was relaxed about accepting Adrian's assistance. He was very confident about what he was doing. In turn, Adrian was really motivated to do a good job. He not only liked Susan, but it felt like he was back doing projects as Adrian Crawley Associates.

o-O-o

Friday 5th May – Ted's funeral

Adrian, Susan, Colin and Michelle went to the crematorium early. Several of the other Acacia Close neighbours slowly began to gather. Susan recognised four family members from her uncle's family – her two second cousins and a couple of mature ladies she took to be distant aunts.

There was also a small group of about five people (two men and three women) who introduced themselves to Susan as former employees of Ted's personal training company. Susan had no expectation of there being any more mourners.

The ceremony was brief and functional. Despite tensions, Susan had invited everyone back to a modest funeral reception in a private room within the George Hotel in the High Street. It had been a long time since it had operated as an actual hotel, but it did a good trade with pensioner lunches, evening meals and funeral receptions. Colin spotted a poster for a karaoke competition but before he could say anything, Michelle said, "Don't you be getting any ideas!"

Susan announced a free bar and soon plates of mixed sandwiches and stock buffet items were brought in.

Adrian went over to the group of former staff. He told them he was Ted's next-door neighbour and asked their names. The trouble was, he couldn't retain all the information and promptly forgot them all apart from a big bloke who looked like a body builder and a small, thin woman with bleached blonde hair. The hunky bloke was called Mike, and the blonde woman was Tracy.

Adrian was unsure how to start the conversation and found himself blurting out, "Bet it was a blow to you all when the company went under."

"Not really," said Mike, "We could see it coming a mile off. He had too many centres on the go, and he was never there when problems occurred. We got wind of financial difficulties about a year ago. Some trainers were lucky and got fixed up in Total Fitness and other big gyms. Others hung on hoping things would improve. But as the better staff left, it became harder for those left behind to keep the ship afloat."

"Were you angry?" asked Adrian.

"Totally hacked off," said Tracy. "We've all got mortgages and some of us have young families too. What are we supposed to do now? OK, so we received statutory redundancy pay but that won't cover anywhere near what we're used to earning."

"So why are you here today?" asked Adrian.

"To be honest, mate, to make sure he's dead and not likely to come back!" said Mike.

Adrian was taken aback by Mike's bluntness and struggled to find something to say.

"Veggie sausage roll, anyone?" Colin butted in carrying a plate of pastries. It broke the tension.

Mike continued, "Look, if you or Teds' niece really want to know the story, you'd best contact Ian Smart. He was the company accountant. Latterly, we referred to him as 'The Head of the Escape Committee'. He got out about a year ago. He's now with one of the big GP practices just down the road – you know, St. Stephens Medical Centre. Practice Manager, I think."

As Adrian left Colin to continue with the small talk, he heard him trot out one of his old gags, "I don't eat many German sausages – they're the wurst kind." There was a smattering of forced laughter.

Adrian went over to rescue Susan from her 'other' family relatives.

The atmosphere was excruciating, and it was a relief when the work colleagues left, closely followed by the Watt family members. The neighbours had not come on to the pub as they had dispersed after the crematorium.

“Glad that’s over with,” said Susan. Michelle helped her to box up the left-over sandwiches and the quartet left, to regroup at Adrian’s house.

“Let’s make a list of what’s left,” suggested Adrian.

“First let’s hope the documents arrive soon, so you can have your uncle’s bank accounts transferred into your name.”

“Second, what do you want to do about the house contents?”

“It can’t be much fun sleeping in a house with all your uncle’s clothes,” ventured Michelle. “I am aware that the James Wilson Mission collects clothing for redistribution to the homeless,” she added. “They’re always after replacement stock.”

"Well," said Susan, "I'm not in a hurry to empty the house. The furnishings are of a decent quality, and I wouldn't mind keeping the property as a furnished bolt hole, at least for the time being. But I'd like to get rid of my Uncle Ted's clothes and his personal stuff. How about all willing volunteers round tomorrow. Is ten thirty, after my run, alright for everyone? Michelle and I can sort the clothes if you two boys start on the shed and garage."

"Boys?" queried Colin, "You need to go to Specsavers."

o-O-o

Colin and Michelle

Colin was a retired qualified accountant. He'd met Michelle while they were both working in the finance department of the local NHS Community and Mental Health Trust. They also had two children, but they'd not returned to Cheshire since completing their degrees.

Colin and Michelle purchased their current house twenty-five years previously, when Acacia Close was first built. They were the first residents, closely followed by Adrian and Pat. Everyone else moved in as each of the eight identical three bedroomed detached properties was completed.

Colin was a very open person and enjoyed a bit of banter with the neighbours. He was the main instigator of the street parties and he and Michelle quite often arranged summer barbeques on the grass triangle in the centre of the close.

After retiring, a couple of years ago, Colin joined the local amenity society whose main aim was to protect the village's green spaces. At the time of joining, Adrian thought this was a bit rich as the eight detached houses in Acacia Close had been built on the site of a small plant nursery.

Michelle was a volunteer with Age Concern. Not only was she a driver for ad hoc hospital visits but she also helped with the 'Meals-on-Wheels' rota every now and again.

If anyone in the close was stuck, the couple would try to help. They were particularly kind to Adrian during Pat's illness.

o-O-o

Saturday 6th May

The next day was bit damp and overcast but it didn't stop operation house clearance. Susan took charge saying there would be three categories: "keep", "charity shop" and "tip." Colin had offered to take all the tip items to the recycling centre in his trailer.

Adrian lifted the garage door and inside, the contents were in a right old mess. "I'm not sure where to start," he said to Colin.

Colin suggested dragging the big stuff out and then sorting the smaller stuff into Susan's three piles.

Out came the lawn mower, an old bike, and half a dozen plastic garden chairs. But when they lifted Ted's ladders out, Adrian's eye was drawn to what appeared to be a muddy footprint on the side of the ladder.

"That's odd", he said, "I'd not noticed that before."

“Probably nothing,” Colin replied, “Ted’s garage is so stuffed and untidy, he probably stood on the ladder edge to reach something near the back.”

Adrian’s imagination went into overdrive as his mind conjured up all sorts of sinister theories. He agreed with Colin that it was probably nothing but a nagging feeling inside prompted him to pull out his mobile phone and take a photograph of the footprint.

The clear-out continued with the “tip” pile growing fastest – old tins of paint, useless lengths of wood, an old George Foreman grill, two more rusty bikes, loads of old plastic plant pots, two half bags of cement which had gone hard, and much, much more.

Ted’s tools were of mixed quality. A rusty saw went in the tip pile as did an old car jack. Anything which still had a legitimate use was put in the “keep” pile.

“Coffee!” shouted Susan.

Adrian and Colin joined "the girls" in the kitchen. Adrian remembered his chat with Mike the personal trainer, who he had met at the funeral and thought Susan may be interested in what he'd said.

"Not a lot we can do about that now," mused Susan. "The company went bust and to be honest, if it were still a going concern, I would have no interest in taking it over."

After a while, Adrain drained his mug and said, "Let's crack on, looks like it's pouring with rain."

"Just a sec, Adrian," said Colin, "What about telling Susan about the footprint?"

Adrian quickly explained what he'd found. "We must have missed it in the commotion immediately after Ted's fall."

"What are you thinking?" asked Susan.

"That Ted didn't fall through overbalancing. Maybe someone booted the ladder."

"A bit Agatha Christie," said Michelle. "Anyway, nobody saw anyone in the close that day and besides, the coroner has ruled that it was accidental death."

"Maybe we should let Olivia know," ventured Susan, "We don't want to be accused of withholding information." With that she rummaged in her handbag and after finding the business card, dialled Olivia's number. It rang out until Susan was invited to leave a voice message.

"This is Susan Watt, from Acacia Close. I'd like to discuss a matter relating to the death of Edward Watt. Please ring me back on this number."

The four went to recommence sorting through Ted's stuff but when Adrian and Colin stepped out of the back door, a mixture of sleet and heavy rain was pouring down. The muddy footprint had now disappeared.

By lunchtime, Adrian and Colin had bagged and boxed up all the stuff for the tip and had replaced all the useful items back in the garage. Meanwhile, Susan and Michelle had put masses of Ted's clothes into bin liners ready to take to the mission.

"A good morning's work," commented Susan.

Just then her mobile phone beeped indicating an incoming call. It was Olivia.

"Hi Liv, it's Susan Watt here. I just wanted to run something past you. It may be nothing, but we've started to do a bit of house clearance. When my neighbours were sorting through the garage, they noticed a footprint on the side of my uncle's ladder and were wondering if it had been kicked over rather than the ladder simply slipping."

There was a stunned silence and it seemed ages before Liv replied, first with an audible sigh. "I thought the coroner's report was pretty clear," she said. "However, I'll pass this to my non-uniform colleagues to look into." She seemed a little distant and less friendly than when they'd met the other day.

"Ah well, I think we did the right thing," said Susan, as the three neighbours left to hurry to their own houses and out of the rain.

o-O-o

Monday 8th May

Susan called round to see Adrian. "There's someone from the police coming round later. Will you be in?"

"Yes, here all day," he replied.

Later, at about 3.45, Susan, and a large man in a raincoat, appeared at Adrian's front door.

"This is Detective Inspector Roberts," introduced Susan, as Adrian showed them both through to his lounge.

D.I Roberts was overweight, if not obese. He had a ruddy complexion and seemed to be short of breath. He plonked himself down into Adrian's favourite armchair with an exhalation of air.

“So, what’s all this about a footprint?” asked DI Roberts.

“Just what Susan told PC Briers,” said Adrian. When we were tidying the garage, we found a footprint on the side of Ted’s aluminium ladder. I was a bit suspicious that someone might have kicked the ladder down. PC Briers did say to contact her if we thought of anything else.”

“Can I have a look at it?” asked the DI.

“The ladder, you mean?” asked Adrain naively before quickly realising he meant the footprint. “Er, no, I’m afraid yesterday’s rain completely washed it off. I took a photo of it though.”

Adrian fumbled in his pocket and painstakingly scrolled through his screen until he located the image. “It’s a bit blurry,” he said, showing it to DI Roberts.

DI Roberts squinted at the image and pulled a face. “Look,” he said, “we don’t like timewasters. That grubby photograph is not what we would regard as evidence. Besides, the coroner has already given a verdict of accidental death. And, right at the moment, we're up to here with amateur sleuths. Ever since that Richard Osman book about the murder club was published, we've been inundated with do-gooders trying to do our job for us."

"So, case closed?" asked Adrian.

"Yup. That's about it, but if it makes you feel any better, I'll take a copy of the image for the files. I need to crack on now and join my colleagues. We've got a major operation down on the Dale Farm Estate. We're really busy at the moment. You were lucky I had a short window to fit in your visit."

With that, DI Roberts had two or three goes at lifting himself from Adrian's chair before shuffling out through the front door and down the path. He sat down heavily in the driving seat of his car. He took a while to find his keys and locate his seat belt before driving off slowly.

Adrian suddenly remembered he was going to download the shoe image on his computer so he could provide DI Roberts with a copy but concluded that if he was that bothered, DI Roberts would have waited while he processed it.

Nevertheless, he did download it and enlarged the image. He printed off an A4 copy for Susan to peruse.

"Oooh," said Susan, "That looks a bit like the sole of a running shoe. In fact, with all those knobbly bits, I'd say it looks like a trail or a fell shoe."

Adrian looked bemused. He thought a sports shoe was a sports shoe and had never considered there were varieties.

"Yes," said Susan, "You run in spikes for cross country races, trail shoes for, well, trail running, road shoes for tarmac and fell shoes for running up and down mountains."

"Who on earth would want to do that?"

"Loads of people, but mainly very strong runners who can run about ten miles with lots of climbing and steep descents. We don't have many fells in

Dartford but here, you seem to be quite handy for North Wales. However, I think we've little or no chance of matching one shoe print to hundreds of runners in Cheshire and beyond!"

"For what it's worth, I'd say the imprint we found on the ladder looked to be a fairly large shoe size, maybe a ten or eleven," added Adrian, "but that doesn't narrow it down much at all."

o-O-o

Tuesday 9th May

Susan called what she referred to as a 'Case Conference' at her uncle's house. The lounge was now looking very presentable with some lived-in touches – fresh flowers and a general air of tidiness The furniture had been rearranged with a couple of older items put outside ready for the tip. She had invited Adrian, Colin and Michelle.

"First item on the agenda is to thank you guys for being so supportive. These last couple of weeks have been a bit strange and so, so, busy. It's great to have neighbours like you."

“Second thing, although the police seem to have gone a bit cool on furthering their investigations, I have an uneasy feeling about my uncle’s fall. I know he didn’t feel like an actual close relative, but he was my blood uncle, and, despite the estrangement, I think my dad would have wanted me to carry on a bit further. Turning over a few more stones, as it were, particularly regarding his business.”

“So, I’ve decided that I’d like to have a chat with Ian Smart, the accountant, and I’m wondering if you, Adrian, would accompany me for moral support?”

Adrian nodded but didn’t interrupt Susan’s flow.

“At some point, I’d like one of us to see if they can get more out of the solicitor, this Mowatt fellow, and possibly look into who may have owned the mysterious training shoe. Once we have all the information, we can present it to DI Roberts. But if our enquiries come to nought, then I’m happy to call it quits.”

"Gosh," said Adrian, "we really are beginning to sound like those characters in the Richard Osman book. I'm up for a chat with the accountant. How about we pop down to St. Stephens Medical Centre in the morning, but not too early!"

"Fine," said Susan, "We'll pick up on the other stuff later."

"I'll do another tip run," added Colin.

o-O-o

Wednesday 10th May

Susan rang Adrian's doorbell ready to drive him to the medical centre. She was somewhat surprised to see Adrian in a smart business suit, white shirt, a regimental-type of diagonally striped tie, and carrying a smart slim, black, briefcase.

"You scrub up well," remarked Susan.

"I thought it may help discussions," Adrian replied.

The Medical Centre car park was congested but Susan managed to squeeze her car into a space round the back near to the garage where the groundsman appeared to keep his ride-on lawn mower. There was also a skip where various bits of redundant equipment had been tossed.

Attached to the side of the garage was a neatly coiled hose reel attached to a tap.

"That must be where they do the colonic irrigation," smirked Susan.

Adrian was taken aback. "You're worse than Colin."

The pair walked into a large and airy, combined open-plan reception area and waiting room.

There were about a dozen people in chairs all facing a TV screen showing a short film about heathy diet, but the sound was off. Most were just looking vacant or thumbing through old magazines.

Adrian marched up to the reception desk purposefully.

The receptionist glanced up from her keyboard and said to him, "If you've got an appointment, you have to log in on the touch screen over there, but if it's a covid booster jab you're after, just go straight up the stairs and report to room 16."

"We would like to see your Practice Manager, Mr Smart."

"Have you got an appointment?"

"No, we haven't, sorry."

"He won't see anyone without an appointment."

"Would you make one for us?"

"Sorry, luvvie, no can do. All appointments must be made online."

Feeling a little exasperated, and with each exchange resulting in an ever-increasing volume, Adrian said, "Look, we're here now and you have the appointment book. Surely you could arrange something."

By now, everyone in the waiting room was finding the conversation far more entertaining than the TV. They were now all facing the reception desk eagerly awaiting what might come next.

"What's the appointment for?" asked the receptionist.

Adrian was sorely tempted to play to the gallery and say in a loud voice, "I would like a doctor to examine these peculiar red spots on my todger," but he thought better of it. Instead, he passed one of his old business cards across the desk and whispered, "We're Private Investigators." Susan shot him a surprised glance which was missed by the receptionist.

That seemed to do the trick. Adrian and Susan were asked to take a seat while the receptionist retreated to a telephone in the back office.

Shortly, a middle-aged man, whom Adrian took to be the Practice Manager appeared. "Like to come through?" he invited.

Once in his office, he introduced himself and shook hands. “I’m Ian Smart,” he said.

“Adrian Crawley, and my associate, Susan.” (Adrian had already planned not to use Susan’s surname in case it raised suspicion).

“Thank you for agreeing to see us. I’ll come straight to the point. We were wondering what you could tell us about Watt and Wyatt, Personal Training Services.”

Ian Smart’s mouth opened with surprise. After a few seconds, he said, “Thank goodness for that. I thought you were here about another patient complaint. Ever since we started encouraging patients to tell us how we performed, we’ve been inundated with people having a go. Chancers.”

“I know all about those,” thought Susan.

“Gosh”, said Ian, “It’s almost a year since I left there, and it’s a long story. Look, I really cannot devote my time here to discuss non-practice matters. I’m very happy to talk to you but I’d much prefer it if we met somewhere neutral.”

“We’re very flexible”, said Susan, not wishing to look like a spare part, “How about Niko’s coffee shop? Saturday afternoon any good? It should be quiet then.”

“That’s fine”, said Ian, “But can we make it Saturday 20th and maybe 2.30?”

The trio shook hands and Ian showed Adrian and Susan back to reception. As he exited, Adrian purposely made eye contact with Mrs Grump, the receptionist. He smiled sarcastically, licked his index finger, and made a large ‘tick’ symbol in the air. The receptionist scowled.

Once back in her car, Susan asked, “How long have we been private investigators?”

“About 15 minutes,” said Adrian. “We needed a way in. I dug out my old business suit and the quasi-regimental tie. I think the word ‘investigations’ on my old business card helped too.”

As they drove back into Acacia Close, the pair were startled by the shocking sight which greeted them.

Lying face downwards on the pavement, in front of his house, was Colin!

“Cripes!” exclaimed Adrian.

“Not another corpse,” screamed Susan.

o-O-o

Deceased Colin?

Susan and Adrian jumped out of the car and rushed over to Colin’s prostrate body. He was making soft grunting noises, and his right shoulder was twitching.

“Colin!” shouted Adrian.

Colin turned over in surprise.

“What?”

"What are you doing down there?" asked Susan, "we thought you were dead!"

Colin knelt up slowly, then stood up. "What does it look like I'm doing? I'm turning off the water at the main stopcock."

Adrian looked quizzical.

"Bit of a long story. Michelle asked me to check the bathroom tap. Hasn't been turning off properly for a while. I suspected it needed a new washer."

"Why didn't you turn the water off at the stop tap under your sink?" asked Adrian, still using his private detective voice.

"Good question. Ours is located behind the dishwasher which I dragged out a bit too vigorously. I'd forgotten that the cold-water feed was a bit short. I ended up pulling it off the dishwasher. Water started gushing out all over the kitchen floor. I managed to plug the pipe with one of those fancy wine bottle corks."

"Why didn't you turn off the house stop cock, stupid?"

"It's jammed solid", replied Colin, "and that's not all. There's about two inches of water all over the kitchen floor right now. D'ya fancy helping me to mop it up before Michelle gets back?"

o-O-o

Friday 12th May

Susan asked Adrian if he'd like to join her at the following day's parkrun. Adrian thought for a moment before saying that he'd go along to watch.

o-O-o

Saturday 13th May

Susan rang his bell at 8.30. Luckily Adrian had set his alarm clock and was ready to spectate.

When they arrived at the park, it was exactly as Susan had described. Yes, there were some very athletic specimens performing all sorts of leg stretches and high knee exercises, but there were additionally what Adrian decided were ordinary looking people, some with dogs on leads and a few pram pushers.

"Why don't you have a go at walking the course", suggested Susan. "It's three laps of roughly one mile. You can pack in after one if it's not for you."

Adrian thought for a bit and concluded that having made the effort to have an early breakfast, he might prefer a bit of a walk as opposed to standing around on the sidelines.

Just before nine o'clock, one of the marshalls summoned any new parkrunners to a briefing to describe the course and check that people had their barcodes with them. Adrian didn't have one as he had only intended spectating. The marshall said that was OK but not to go through the finishing funnel. Adrian did not intend reaching even the halfway point, never mind the finish!

Susan made her way to the front of the runners leaving Adrian, and several other mature men and women, in the care of the 'Tail Walker' – a small, blonde lady.

Adrian thought her face looked familiar and after searching through his grey matter, realised she had been at Ted's funeral.

The Race Director made a few announcements before counting down 3-2-1, Go!

Nothing happened for about 20 seconds and then everyone stepped forwards. Adrian found himself in a mixed group of about a dozen walkers. The fast runners had disappeared into the distance, but he could see a long snake of people in front of him progressing at various speeds. He soon settled into a steady rhythm.

The other walkers looked a bit more experienced and soon he was on his own at the back with the tail walker.

"It's my first time," admitted Adrian.

"Don't worry. I'm Tracy. I'm your volunteer tail walker for today."

"I know you," said Adrian, "We met briefly at Ted Watt's funeral. I was his next-door neighbour. You told me you used to work for Ted."

They approached the first pink jacketed marshall who was ringing a bell and giving loud encouragement.

"What was your role in Ted's company?" Adrian ventured.

"I was initially taken on as a personal trainer but when Watt found out that I had a bookkeeping background, he moved me to the office. I worked with the accountant doing a bit of invoicing and processing incoming bills, at least when we had the money to pay our suppliers. After Ian left, I was on my own, grappling with everything, including payroll. And that wasn't the only grappling that was going on. I felt very vulnerable being alone in the back office. Watt was a smarmy so-and-so. It started with lewd and suggestive comments. Once he groped me – slowly ran his hand over my bottom while I was standing at the photocopier. I shouted, "Gerroff" in a very loud voice and after that he didn't try anything.

I should have resigned there and then but I was so desperate for money, I stuck it out. It was terrible. I had creditors ringing every day demanding payment. I was told to think up excuses like, 'the cheque is being prepared as we speak' or, 'we had a small fire in the office, yesterday'. I was instructed not to pay unless we received a solicitor's letter. What made matters worse was Ted was withdrawing large amounts of cash for personal use which he described as 'dividends' and then shortly afterwards flying over to Ireland for a couple of days. In the end, it was a huge relief when the firm closed down. I hated working there and I hated that man."

"Oh, dear", muttered Adrain. "What happened to the other partner, Mr Wyatt?"

"Pete, you mean. Not sure. When I first joined the company, he seemed to be in the back office. We didn't see much of him at all. One day we heard that he'd left."

By now the front runners were overtaking them and soon Susan ran past giving Adrian an encouraging shout out.

“We’re approaching the end of lap one,” said Tracy. “How are you feeling?”

“OK”, said Adrian, “but I think that will be enough for my first attempt. Thanks for looking after me.”

“That’s fine. Sorry for the outpouring but it’s good to get these things off your chest. I hope you’ll come next week. Maybe two laps next time.”

“Will you be here?”

“Yes, I’m here most Saturday mornings, but I’ll be running. There will be a different tail walker next week.”

Adrian discovered that the end of the first lap was next to the finishing funnel, so he joined about thirty supporters and spectators to wait for Susan to finish. He was amazed that the first runner arrived in a time of 17 minutes, roughly the same time that he’d taken to do one lap.

Soon, the runners were approaching the finish in droves. He spied Susan making a great effort to overtake another runner just before the line.

After handing in her finishing token, Susan met up with Adrian and as they walked back to Susan's car, Adrian gave Tracy a wave as she walked past on her lap two, accompanying a couple of older women.

"What did you think? asked Susan.

"Surprisingly good," replied Adrian. "I got on better than I thought. Had an interesting chat too. Did you recognise Tracy from the funeral?"

On the drive home, Adrian filled Susan in on their discussion.

"Do you think Tracy could be a murderer?" suggested Susan. "You know, the training shoe and the bad experience with my uncle?"

"I don't think so," said Adrian, "she is very petite, and I noticed she has particularly small feet."

o-O-o

During the week, Adrian applied online for his parkrun barcode. After he'd printed it off and, in typical Adrian style, laminating it, he couldn't resist popping next door to show Susan.

o-O-o

Saturday 20th May

The weather on the following Saturday morning was glorious. Adrian was up early and waiting outside his front door when Susan appeared.

Arriving at the park, it was the same routine as the previous week but as Tracy had warned him, there was a different tail walker – a sprightly man who looked much older than himself.

"3-2-1 Go!" shouted the Race Director.

This time, Adrian knew what to expect and set off with a purposeful stride. Nevertheless, the faster walkers gradually pulled ahead leaving him once more with the tail walker.

"Is this your first time?" he asked.

"Second actually."

"Well, I'm Keith. I sometimes marshall, I sometimes do the tail walker job and sometimes I even walk/jog. I'm 77, so my times are becoming slower but at least I'm staying active."

"I'm Adrian and I'm about 20 years your junior. In just one sentence you've inspired me to complete the course today!"

As the pair continued with their walk and talk, it transpired that Keith was a retired personnel manager. His daughter, son-in-law and three grandchildren were parkrun regulars as was their family dog, Boo. At the entrance to the finishing tunnel and about to commence their second lap, Adrian was pleased to note that the front runners had not overtaken them this time, indicating a quicker pace than last week.

On lap two, they were overtaken by runners including Susan. Many gave Adrian verbal encouragement. As he approached the finish on lap two, he abandoned all thoughts of packing in early and started his third and final lap. Susan, who had already finished ran on to catch him up. "This is great, Adrian."

Adrian, Keith, and Susan eventually reached the finish funnel. Adrian was amazed that there were so many people clapping him in. "Par for the course," said Keith, "We're like a family here."

Adrian pulled out his shiny new barcode and the marshall scanned it.

"Home for a coffee next," he said to Keith, "and thank you for looking after me."

"Don't forget we are meeting someone at two," reminded Susan.

o-O-o

Adrian was feeling tired but inwardly smug at having walked three miles before coffee. Things became even better when his computer pinged, and he received an email with his result. There was his name, listed as a 'first timer'. His time was 54 minutes and 40 seconds. He was 32nd in his age group but was not the last to finish as Keith the tail walker was listed as having crossed the line after him.

But gosh, he snoozed well after his lunch and was awoken by his doorbell. It was Susan, accompanied by Colin. They'd come to collect Adrian for their scheduled Saturday afternoon meeting with Ian Smart, the accountant.

"I had this thought that as we'll be discussing accounts, it may help discussions if Colin came along," reasoned Susan.

"How are we getting to the coffee shop," asked Adrian.

"Walking, of course."

After his morning's efforts, Adrian would have preferred a lift in Susan's BMW but was gradually falling for her enthusiasm for a heathy lifestyle.

On the way, Susan asked, "Are we going to come clean about not being private detectives?"

“I think so,” Adrian replied. “I think it will help discussions if you explain about being your Uncle Ted’s niece.”

“Private detectives?” exclaimed Colin in disbelief. “Gumshoes? You two?”

“Means to an end,” said Adrian. “Besides, I’m not in my private eye suit today and we’d have to think up a story as to why Colin was tagging along.”

o-O-o

The trio arrived at Nico’s café just as Ian Smart was approaching from the other direction. He seemed surprised to be outnumbered and by Adrian’s Saturday afternoon dress sense.

“Don’t worry, we will explain,” said Susan as they found an empty table in the far corner.

The waitress took their order – a fruit tea for Susan and three Lattes for the men. Adrian fancied a chocolate flapjack but resisted the temptation. After all, he was an athlete now.

“I’ll start,” said Susan.

“I have to come clean and say that we’re not Private Detectives. That was necessary to get past Lotte Klebb the other day, and to secure contact with you. I am actually Ted Watt’s niece and sole surviving relative. These two reprobates are my neighbours, Adrian, and Colin. They are helping me to sort out my Uncle Ted’s affairs. I’m assuming you know that he died about three weeks ago?”

“Gosh,” said Ian. “Well, I’m quite relieved about the Private Detective thing and yes, I had heard on the grapevine that Ted had fallen off a ladder or something and had died in hospital.”

The drinks arrived.

“We don’t really know much about Ted’s business other than it went into compulsory liquidation a few months ago and that it was run as a personal fitness company,” said Adrian.

"Well, I'll fill you in with what I know. Have you got five hours?" he joked.

Ian continued, "I was employed in the accounts department of Pristine Publishing. They're a fairly big organisation turning out the glossy mags you see around the patch. Not quite Cheshire Life you understand but high-end advertisements and pictures of society balls etc. Things went a bit pear shaped when the advertisers started taking less and less space. In the end the company made my post redundant. 'We're going to have to let you go,' they said. As I'm only part qualified, I struggled to find another job until I saw an advert for an accountant for Watt and Wyatt Personal Training Services. Ted Watt interviewed me and offered me the job.

On my first day, I realised I'd made a huge mistake. The accounts were in a right mess and a couple of the staff asked me what I was thinking about by joining such a terrible firm. They didn't speak too highly of Ted Watt at all, saying he came in late, liked a drink at lunchtime and had these fits of temper. But I needed the money and knew I had to persevere. There were very few other opportunities out there at the time.

I had a young lady called Tracy to assist me. She was totally unqualified but could do basic bookkeeping and I showed her the ins and outs of payroll.

I quickly got to understand a bit more about the company. Apparently, it started out as a one-man business by a certain Peter Wyatt who was a very good personal trainer. He had the old Mini-Mart premises in the High Street and was doing OK. One day, Ted Watt called in thinking it was retail outlet selling weights for home use and the pair got talking. Your uncle somehow persuaded Pete that they could make lots of money if Pete's business expanded and benefitted from the 'economies of scale'. (Colin nodded).

"It all went well to begin with but after expanding to two gyms then three, then four and so on, it all went a bit 'Rolling Stones'," continued Ian.

"Couldn't get any satisfaction?" smirked Colin.

Ian ignored the awful quip and continued, "Well, if you don't know about the Rolling Stones, there are plenty of books describing what happened. It was Brian Jones who started the band. He recruited the other four. He was the leader and secured all of the band's early radio broadcasts. However, as time went on, he found himself gradually sidelined by the others. After contributing less and less, he was eventually sacked. He died in his swimming pool a couple of weeks later, aged 27.

It was a very similar story with Peter. His business model was good – take over a vacant shop, secure low rent and possibly a twelve-month business rates holiday. The council hate having empty shops on their high street.

Peter's initial gym had plenty of clients and his overheads were relatively low once he'd purchased a set of weights, some medicine balls and some Pilates mats. He employed just one other person to lead the classes and he took the one-to-one sessions.

I think the company expanded far too quickly. When I joined, they had eighteen premises and employed 70 odd staff. Somewhere along the line, Ted Watt transferred the assets to a limited company to protect his personal wealth should anything go wrong. This wasn't what Peter wanted. He got out just before the company went limited, but Ted retained Pete's name as he had a really good reputation locally."

"What happened to Peter Wyatt?" asked Adrian.

"Nobody really knows. As far as I know, he never revisited the premises. Ted didn't mention him. I guessed he'd either got another job in another part of the country, emigrated, or even died."

"And then," prompted Adrian.

"My job became harder and harder as the debts mounted up. You cannot take on staff and buy equipment until there is sufficient income from the rest of the business. Ted just kept on taking on new premises and extending the company's overdraft with the bank. And worse, he was taking far too much out of the business for himself, way over what a normal salary would be.

What did it for me was when the Inland Revenue came calling. In order to pay the staff, the tax and NI contributions hadn't been paid over to them for a couple of years.

I just had to find another job or be tainted with fraud. Luckily, the vacancy at the Health Centre came up and I nailed it at the first interview. Dropped young Tracy in it though. She wasn't an accountant but was left holding the baby. It was hard when the creditors used to ring up and she had to think up excuses. I felt really sorry for one of the suppliers – a family business who supplied office equipment. Ted couldn't get purchaser credit from the big boys like Ryman's, so he took advantage of those guys. He took delivery of new desks, office chairs and white boards and then wouldn't pay their invoices.

And did you know that Ted had a house which he let out to students? (Susan shook her head).

After I left, I kept in contact with Tracy and one of the trainers called Mike. Turns out, when things became really bad and the bank were chasing Ted because of his overdraft, he took out a second mortgage on the student house to placate the bank. What did they do? They said, 'Thank you very much' and immediately closed the company's bank account. And that was it. The Inland Revenue instigated the compulsory liquidation, and the staff were all out of work. So sudden."

Ian sat back and drained his latte.

The other three were stunned into silence.

Colin was the first to react. "I guess the Inland Revenue were the principal creditors but after they'd taken what was owing, there wasn't much left for anyone else. What happened to all the assets, Ian?"

"I heard the bailiffs went round all the premises and seized anything that moved – filing cabinets, gym equipment and desks – the lot. They were auctioned off near here. I heard that stuff was going for a fraction of its normal value. Mike did well. Have you met Mike? (the three nodded). He bought a load of gear and set himself up in one of the old shops and is now doing very nicely. It's a one-man business a bit like what Peter Wyatt started a few years back."

"I met Mike at the funeral", said Adrian, "He didn't seem very keen on Ted."

"Not very keen? They hated each other's guts. Mike was an excellent trainer, and the customers all loved him. He brought a lot of revenue into the business, but Ted never acknowledged it. When the income across the whole company started to fall, Ted tried to trim Mike's wages, but Mike stood up to him. I think he was the only one who did. He also told Ted to back off when Tracy told him that Ted had groped her bottom."

"What a dreadful place to work, Ian," ventured Susan.

"Yes, awful," added Adrian, "I'd never have guessed it from the way Ted used to brag about the business during our over-the-garden-fence chats."

"Thank you for being so frank, Ian" added Susan, "And thank you for giving up part of your Saturday."

"No problem," said Ian. "Thanks for the coffee. Nice café, this."

With that, Ian shook hands with everyone before he left the trio to discuss what he'd told them.

"The plot thickens," said Adrian. "It's beginning to sound less and less like an accident."

"I think we need another case conference," said Susan. "How about the four of us have meal out on Wednesday?"

o-O-o

Wednesday evening 24th May

After the quartet had been served their after-meal coffees, Susan opened the discussion. "Maybe we should summarise what we've got so far and then plan our next moves."

Susan started with the training shoe print which suggested that the cause of death may not have been accidental. She added that if they were able to find a suspect with a motive and an opportunity to knock Ted off his ladder, they could then provide the police with the facts. In the meantime, she wondered about Mike, the former employee and one who hated her uncle.

Ian Smart had seemed very genuine and had provided useful background information. From his description of what had happened to her uncle's former business partner, Peter Wyatt, Susan was keen to track him down if only to eliminate him from their shortlist of suspects.

Susan wondered about Mike, the disgruntled body builder who's stood up to her uncle. Maybe worth a further chat. Then there was the office equipment supplier. Would he seek revenge for being so badly ripped off? Finally, there was the rude and abrupt Company Secretary, Neil Mowatt. What more did he know?

"Blimey," said Adrian, "that's quite a shopping list. Suppose Colin and I pop down to visit the equipment supplier then after that, maybe we could smooth talk Mike the body builder for more information. That just leaves that solicitor fellow. He's only spoken to you Susan, so you and I can put on our Private Detective suits and see where our enquiries lead us."

"Sounds like a plan," said Susan.

"There are still about half a dozen bags of Ted's clothes," added Michelle. Maybe I could take them to the mission sometime."

"In the meantime," announced Susan, "I have relocated to Acacia Avenue for the remainder of my six-month sabbatical, so you'll be seeing a lot more of me. Also, I've joined the local running club so don't be surprised if you see me coming and going in my sports kit."

o-O-o

Thursday, 25th May

Adrian telephoned the Health Centre. The voice at the other end did not sound like the grumpy receptionist. He asked to be put through to Ian Smart who answered straight away.

"Ian, it's Adrian Crawley here. I won't take up your time. I just wanted to ask you the name of the office equipment firm who supplied Watt and Wyatt."

"No problem at all, Adrian. The company trades as A1 Office Supplies. They are situated on the Cromwell Business Park on Tower Road. The office and reception face the main road and the warehouse is around the back. The main man is John Cooper but the sales rep who dealt with Ted Watt was called Dave Williams. Good luck with your enquiries."

Later that morning, Colin appeared at Ted's front door dressed in a business suit which seemed to have shrunk in direct proportion to the number of years he had been retired. "Do I look OK?" he asked Adrian. "Yes, but let me do the talking," he replied.

The pair used Colin's car as it was a bit posher than Adrian's. They parked in the visitor's parking bay and entered the reception area. Although there was no one at the desk, there was a small notice which invited visitors to ring a 'hotel-reception' type of bell. Colin couldn't resist ringing it with that annoying football crowd clapping rhythm.

"Are you alright there?" asked the young girl who came through a door at the back.

"Yes, perfectly all right, thank you," replied Adrian who was forever irritated by this inane question, usually spoken by a juvenile who had not been properly trained in customer service.

Colin said nothing.

"Is there anything I can help you with?" asked the teenager.

"That's a bit better," thought Adrian.

"We'd like to see Mr. Cooper, please."

"John or Freddie?"

"The owner, please."

"John then. I'm afraid he's out for most of today. Would you like Freddie?"

"Is Dave Williams around?"

"Dave? Yes, he's in the back office catching up with his paperwork."

"It's rather important that we speak with him," said Adrian sliding his business card across the desk and lowering his voice. "We are Private Investigators."

"OK. Right. I'll tell him you're here."

The girl disappeared through the door behind her. She reappeared from a door at the side of reception marked 'private'. "Like to pop through?" she asked.

Adrian and Colin stepped through into a small interview-type room with a large table and about half a dozen chairs. There was a flip chart in the corner with some business buzzwords scrawled on the top sheet. 'This month's targets', 'Push the new office chairs' and 'Take a helicopter view' were a few Colin remembered.

A smartly dressed man appeared. He was in a crisp white shirt and was wearing a tie with what appeared to be a company logo on it. There was a strong smell of Old Spice after shave. He shook hands firmly with first Adrian and then Colin. As he did so, he said, "Dave Williams, Head of Sales. How are you?"

Dave sat down opposite the pair.

Adrian began. "Thank you for taking time out of what must be a busy day for you. We won't take up too much of your time. We are from Adrian Crawley Associates, Private Investigators. I am Adrian Crawley, and this is my associate, Colin Wilkinson." (He was tempted to introduce Colin as 'Colin Spade', but he didn't want to set Colin off).

“We are looking into the affairs of Watt and Wyatt Personal Training Services Limited. We understand that your company supplied them with office equipment.”

Dave sat there waiting for the next bit.

“We were dismayed to learn that Watt and Wyatt went into enforced receivership. That must have been awful for everyone here.”

Dave paused before answering. “I don’t think you are speaking to the right person. I am the sales manager. I sell desks, chairs and most other pieces of office equipment. If I hit my targets, I get paid. And if I get paid, my wife is happy. I don’t get involved in what goes on at the next level. I think you’d be better speaking to John Cooper.”

“How many are on your sales team?” asked Colin.

“Err, actually, there’s just me. Head of Sales is a bit of a con. We are a small family firm. I handle most of the sales myself.”

“So, you dealt with Watt and Wyatt,” pressed Adrian.

Dave shifted uneasily in his seat.

“That’s a pretty obvious question for a Private Investigator to ask, isn’t it? I’ve just said I am the sales department of one person.”

“Must have been a bit of a rollercoaster having nailed a big contract only for it to come down like a ton of bricks a few months later?”

“Look, it’s not my job to talk company stuff even to investigators. I’m sorry, but you’ll need to see John. He should be back later.”

“Just one more thing, and you can get back to what you were doing. Were you, or was anyone else at the company, angry when Watt and Wyatt went under?”

Adrian’s question touched a raw nerve.

“We were all shellshocked. It was a very lucrative contract for us. We recently heard that after the

Inland Revenue grabbed what they were due there was nothing left for the creditors. It was a harsh lesson to us all, but we'll bounce back."

Dave got up again and shook hands before going out, closing the door gently behind him.

"I don't think he would do it," said Colin. "Too loyal."

Adrian got up and went back to the reception desk. He rang the bell again but before the receptionist could ask, "Are you alright there" for a second time, Adrian asked when Mr. Cooper senior was due back.

The teenager looked at an A4, handwritten, book on the desk. She glanced at the clock and said, "In about half an hour."

"Mind if we wait?", asked Adrian.

"No problem. Help yourselves to coffee." The receptionist pointed to a machine in the corner. Adrian pressed the button for a latte. It was disgusting.

"We've still to see that dodgy solicitor," said Colin, "and have another chat with Mike, the body builder."

"All in good time," replied Adrian.

At around five o'clock, they heard a car door slam just outside where they were sitting. As a large man burst through the outside door, they heard the receptionist say, "There are two fellas waiting to see you."

Colin and Adrian reeled back slightly as this huge man stormed into the room. He must have been 6'6" and almost as wide. He had what Colin later described as a "lived-in" face with scowl lines above his nose.

"You waitin' to see me?" he boomed. "What's it about?"

"Mr. Cooper," began Adrian, "We are Private Investigators looking into the recent affairs of Watt and Wyatt Personal Training Services Limited." Adrian slid one of his business cards across the table. “We really don’t want to take up too much of your time - you have a business to run.”

Colin took over as, like Susan, he didn’t want to appear like a spare part.

“We’re aware of your contract to supply office equipment to Ted Watt and we are sorry that things turned sour when his company went into receivership. But is there anything you can tell us about Watt and Wyatt?”

John Cooper pulled up a chair and sat down.

“It’s all water under the bridge now,” he began in a surprisingly calm and softly spoken voice. “At the time, my son and I debated whether we wanted the contract. They didn’t have a good credit rating on Experion, but Freddie persuaded me to go with it. We smelled a rat when our invoices weren’t paid on time. Whenever we followed up why we’d not been paid, some slip of girl in their accounts office just gave us stupid excuses which even a 10-year-old would see through. In the end we started to take legal action, but the Inland Revenue beat us to it. We joined the list of creditors but knew we had little or no chance of even 5p in the pound. Freddie spotted the Liquidator's notice about the auction in the local rag and managed to bid successfully for most of the gear we'd supplied. Got it at a really good price. We've advertised all of the furniture and planning boards on our website, so we should recover over half the money."

"You must be very bitter," suggested Colin.

John Cooper smirked.

"Listen son, in this business you cannot afford to be bitter. You win some, you lose some. You have to roll with the punches. It'll take a few months but we're still in business and we'll get over it."

Adrian and Colin were taken aback by his pragmatic and calm approach especially after they initially thought they were dealing with a short-tempered hardcase business owner.

"Look, I've got a desk full of stuff to get on with. Is that all?" Adrian nodded, went to shake hands, but Mr. Cooper was already halfway out of the door.

Back in the car, Colin asked, “What do you think? Suspects?”

“I wouldn’t have said so,” replied Adrian. “There was no animosity there whatsoever.”

o-O-o

Friday 26th May

After he’d allowed Adrian his waking up time and his first scan of his newspaper, Colin ambled across to his house and rang his bell.

“We said we’d visit Mike the body builder today,” said Colin.

“Aye, OK, I’ll just pop my shoes on.”

Adrian said they'd be walking because parking may be difficult and besides, he was on a new health kick.

"So, we're not private eyes today," mooted Colin.

"No point. Mike will probably remember us from Ted's funeral."

As the pair set off, they discussed how they would approach Mike but, in the end, decided to "busk it" – a speaker's term for when the presenter has not prepared his or her spiel.

When they arrived at the shop-cum-training centre, they could see Mike with a female client and in a cowardly sort of way, decided to spend five minutes window shopping. On their return, Mike was overseeing the same client who by this time was lying on her back, on a gym bench, pushing a bar and weights above her torso.

They took a deep breath and went in.

"Be with you shortly, gents, just take a seat," said Mike.

Adrian and Colin sat in a small waiting area. Looking round they noticed a timetable of classes on the wall. There were numerous pieces of sports equipment neatly laid out, either on the floor or on racks attached to the wall. A large notice explained safety precautions and the rear door had 'Fire Exit' above it. There were some certificates behind the counter. They looked impressive but were too far away for Adrian to read. On the low table in front of them were various sports magazines. Adrian formed the view that this was a professionally run operation.

After about five minutes, Mike said, "OK, Jenny. That'll do for today. You're making really good progress. Same time next week?"

"Thanks," said the girl (whom Adrian now knew was called 'Jenny') before she started to put on a green coloured sweatshirt. It had a parkrun logo on the front of it and a large '250' on the back.

Adrian couldn't resist commenting.

"I do the parkrun," he said, half expecting some sort of "wow" moment.

"That's good," said Jenny," I do one every Saturday, sometimes here and sometimes further afield. Right now, I'm working on my A to Z of parkruns."

Adrian nodded but his face told Jenny that he had no clue as to what she was referring to.

Jenny helped him out. "It's where you complete a parkrun using every letter in the alphabet. Not too far from here we've got Birkenhead, Chester, and Delamere. I did Aberystwyth when I was on holiday. Just a couple to go, though I think I'd need to visit The Netherlands for 'Z'."

"What is the '250' on your hoodie," asked Colin. (Adrian didn't know that either and was glad that Colin had asked the question).

"Oh that. You can wear one of these once you've completed 250 parkruns."

Adrain nodded sagely.

“How many are you up to?” she asked Adrian.

“Oooh, heading towards fifty,” he grossly exaggerated, not wishing to sound like an absolute beginner.

“Good for you, keep it up. Right, must be off. See you in a week, Mike.” And with that, Jenny left the premises.

“How can I help?” said Mike, wondering why two potential clients, both older, and flabbier than usual, had darkened his doorway.

“Well,” said Adrian, you probably don’t remember us, but we met briefly at Ted Watt’s funeral a week or so ago.”

“I remember now”, said Mike, “all those tasteless vegetarian nibbles and crap jokes,” he said looking at Colin.

“Well,” ventured Adrian, not sure how to begin, “You gave us a pretty hard-hitting description of Ted and his company at the funeral, but we wondered if there was any more to tell. We've spoken to the accountant, Ian Smart, and his assistant, Tracy. We also had a chat with the people at A1 Office Supplies."

"What's it got to do with you?" said Mike in a distinctly harsh change of tone.

Colin decided to help Adrian out.

"Look", he said, "As we told you at his funeral, we knew Ted quite well as we are, or rather were, both immediate neighbours. The picture of Ted which is being painted by a number of people is different to the Ted we knew. Ted's niece, Susan Watt, is keen to establish which Ted it was that she cremated. She's asked us to make a few informal enquiries on her behalf."

Mike didn't say anything for a while.

Then, trying to control the speed and timbre of his voice, spat out, "If you two are suggesting that I had anything to do with Ted falling off that ladder, you are barking up the wrong tree. I was one of many who strongly disliked Ted but there's no way I would use GBH to settle any scores. You should look further afield starting with that shady solicitor character in Chester, Neil Mowatt."

"Yes, we will be," said Colin. "It's important that we speak to all the key players. Have you actually met Neil Mowatt?"

"No, I never did, though I'd know him if I saw him in the street. He used to pop in to see Ted regularly. My training room overlooked the car park. From what I've heard, and I know it is only hearsay, he is not a very honest solicitor, always doing dodgy deals."

For once, Colin was particularly serious, and Adrian was relieved there were no silly jokes spouting from his mouth, so he let Colin continue.

"Our position is this, Mike. Susan Watt is Ted's niece and immediate next of kin. She's moved up north on a temporary basis while she sorts out Ted's estate. She has accepted our offer of assistance with the unending piles of forms and paperwork. But she also wants to make sure, for her deceased dad's sake, that any doubts about

Ted's death are cleared up. There's probably nothing sinister in his fall and the coroner has logged it as accidental death but we just need to speak to various people to find out a bit more about Ted and his company."

That soliloquy seemed to do the trick. Mike had calmed down and was now conversing with them as 'Mr. Reasonable'.

"Well," said Mike, I think you need to tread carefully. What were you planning?"

It was Adrian's turn to come clean now.

"I have been passing myself off as a Private Investigator recently. It is not a lie as I already have my own business carrying out commercial investigations, though usually as an auditor."

Mike stopped him there. "I don't think homespun, amateur, sleuthing would fool Mowatt for one minute. What exactly are you hoping to achieve?" he asked.

"Did he have a motive to knock Ted off his ladder for one," said Adrian.

"And did he hate Ted enough to want to do it," added Colin.

"You'd need to be a bit more subtle than that," suggested Mike. "Why don't you take Susan Watt along with you. She can ask him to talk her through how the company ended up being compulsorily liquidated and then see how things develop?" suggested Mike. "The trouble is, he may not wish to play ball, or he may do a runner."

Adrian and Mike could see the cogs turning in Mike's brain.

"You two couldn't punch your way out of a wet paper bag. You'd be better if you had some muscle with you. Thursday morning is normally my admin day when I send out invoices, do my banking and catch up with my emails but I'd be prepared to accompany you providing I was back here by say, 12.30, or one o'clock at the latest."

"Would four be a bit overwhelming?" asked Adrian.

"Yes, definitely. Leave Tonto, here, back at the ranch. With Susan there, it may be less threatening. I can just lean against a wall near the door to put him off thinking about slipping away. I wouldn't have a speaking part; I'd leave that to you and Susan. You could say I am your driver."

"This is sounding promising. Should we try to make an appointment or just take a chance and barge into his office?" asked Adrian, realising he had now surrendered the lead to Mike, but pleased to be compared to The Lone Ranger.

"We've got to know he'll be in his office, otherwise it's a wasted trip. Does Susan Watt have access to Ted's diaries? If so, that would identify the days when Ted went over to see him and may give us a clue as to the best day of the week to find him in. Before driving over there, Susan could phone him up to make sure he's in but hang up as soon as he answers."

"Great plan, Kimmo Sabi," said Colin taking the Tonto description a bit too far. "Can we get back to you once we've checked with Susan?"

"No problem, any more questions?"

"Just one" said Colin, "Why did The Lone Ranger dispense with Tonto's services?"

Adrian and Mike looked skywards. "Cos The Lone Ranger discovered that when translated, Kimmo Sabi meant scumbag."

Mike's next client was coming through the door as Colin and Adrian left.

The pair couldn't wait to update Susan but when they reached Acacia Close, they could see that Ted's house was in darkness. Any updates would need to wait.

o-O-o

Saturday 27th May

When Susan called for Adrian at 08.30, he was beaming. He told Susan that he was looking forward to his third parkrun and was determined to complete the full course again.

"I've got loads to tell you," said Adrian, once in the car, "but it may be best to speak over a coffee after the run."

At the park, Adrian knew the drill and he even tried a few legs swings, hoping to give the illusion that he wasn't a total novice anymore. He'd no idea what he was doing – he simply copied a few of the other runners.

When the Race Director had finished her briefing and set everyone off, Adrian started at a steady pace. This time, he pulled ahead of the tail walker who was someone different again to the previous two weeks.

In the end, he was pleased with his time – 50:32, just over his 50-minute target and a four-minute improvement on the previous week.

After a shower, he popped round to see Susan. He was pleased to see that she'd acquired a proper coffee machine. It took two mugs worth of coffee for Adrian to fill Susan in with their conversations both at the office equipment supplier and with 'Big Mike'.

"It's sounding like Ted's fall is turning out to be a careless accident after all. But I'm game to accompany you to see this solicitor chap on Thursday. Maybe we should offer to buy Mike his lunch."

"Won't work," said Adrian, he has to back for 12.30, or one o'clock at the latest."

Susan followed Mike's suggestion by digging out Ted's diary. It was very easy to spot the meetings between Ted and Neil Mowatt. Always in the morning and usually on a Tuesday or a Thursday. Adrian gave Mike a quick ring but left a message on his answerphone. They'd pick him up the following Thursday at 10.30.

o-O-o

Thursday 1st June

"I'm not really looking forward to this," ventured Susan.

"Let's just see how it goes," reassured Adrian.

Susan rang the solicitor's landline.

"Neil Mowatt," came the reply. Susan said, "Sorry wrong number," before pressing the cancel button.

They picked up Mike from his studio/gym, as arranged and drove over to Chester. Neil's office was in a small business complex containing serviced offices. The building was on the fringes of the city, near to the canal and joy of joys, it had free visitor parking.

The trio approached the receptionist, who was a young man who appeared to be looking after about 25 different small businesses.

"We're here to see Neil Mowat," said Adrian.

"First floor, room 3. I'll buzz him to tell him you're here," he replied.

"It's OK, he knows we're coming, we'll just go straight up."

Adrian straightened his tie and jacket before giving a firm knock on the door and going straight in followed by Susan and finally Mike. The solicitor looked startled.

Before he could say anything, Adrian introduced himself and presented his card. He introduced Susan as Ted's niece and immediate next of kin.

Neil Mowatt still hadn't said anything.

Susan went next. "I've recently moved from Kent on a temporary basis while I sort out my uncle's estate. I've been speaking to various people to try find out a bit more about his company and why it went bust. I'm hoping you'd be able to help me."

"And 'oo's 'e?" the solicitor asked, jabbing his finger in Mike's direction but clearly not recognising him as a former employee.

Mike had parked himself on a chair next to the door.

“He’s just our driver,” said Adrian.

“You’ve got a cheek,” said Neil, “I am a very busy man” he said, waving his right hand to piles and piles of files, strewn on tables and across the floor.

“We won’t take up any more time than is strictly necessary,” said Susan. “You were the Company Secretary of Watt and Wyatt, and we wondered what on earth went wrong to what we understand was a successful, medium sized business”.

“I think I must ask you to leave,” he said.

“Hang on, said Adrian,” There’s no hidden agenda here, you know. Miss Watt just wants to know what went wrong.”

“Five minutes,” he replied, before continuing, “Ted and I go back a long way. We met at the rugby club. Over the years, I’d done a lot of work for him, mainly sorting out lease agreements. Two years ago, he said he wanted to convert the business from a private company into a limited company and to transfer the assets across. He needed to have a named Company Secretary for the Companies House application and asked if I'd do it. I was very reluctant as that would make me liable to submit annual accounts and I'm not an accountant. However, I owed Ted a few favours, so I signed the papers and that was that. I did meet Ted at his office regularly but that was to deal with other matters. I should have taken more interest in the company's fortunes but didn't. It took me by surprise when everything went pear shaped."

"You didn't attend Ted's funeral," said Adrian.

"Never do. Hate them. Frank Sinatra was famous for not going to funerals."

"Did you dislike him?"

"Don't be ridiculous. We were good mates, drinking buddies and went on lads' weekends from time to time."

"Do you know if he left a will? asked Susan, "I couldn't find one."

"No idea. I suspect not. He always said he felt like he'd live forever. Probably never occurred to him."

"Do you know how we can contact Peter Wyatt?" asked Susan.

"Sorry. No idea where he is now. He disappeared after he had a row with Ted Watt. Pete wasn't at all happy with the direction Ted was taking the company. In the end he just walked out. He could have claimed half the equity and half the assets, but it was like he just wanted to wash his hands of it. I've not seen nor heard of him since. Pity. He was a nice man."

Susan and Adrian looked at each other blankly. They could think of nothing further to say, other than "Thank you, that's been helpful," before slinking out.

The trio said nothing until they were outside.

"I think we have about 30 minutes before we need to get you back, Mike. Should we grab a coffee?"

“Sure”, said Mike, “Old Harkers Bar is just a short walk along the towpath. They serve good coffee too.”

They’d just joined the towpath when Susan’s phone rang. It was Michelle.

“Hi Susan. Not urgent but I’ve been in touch with the mission, and they’d like us to drop off the clothes next Tuesday.”

Whoosh!

Before Susan had time to reply, a young lad on a bike rode aggressively towards her and grabbed her phone out of her hand before pedalling off quickly. Susan reacted almost immediately, spinning round and sprinting after him. At first, the lad was able to gain ground on Susan, but the towpath was busy with anglers casting their lines and mothers pushing buggies. Susan maintained her fast pace and caught up with him where the towpath opened up near to a grassy patch. When Susan got alongside him, she shoulder-charged the lad on to the grass. He lost his grip on her phone which landed a few yards in front. Susan ran on to retrieve it. As she turned to run back, she stomped on the bike's front wheel and then the rear one, breaking several spokes on each and rendering it unrideable.

"Impressive," said Mike when she reached him.

There was a loud splash as the lad threw the now wrecked bike into the canal.

Over coffee, Susan asked the other two what they thought.

"The opposite of what I expected," said Mike, "He didn't seem to hold any grudges towards Ted, what do you think Ades?"

"Please don't call me 'Ades'. I used to get that a lot at school but it's since acquired connotations of 'Aids' and I hate it."

Adrian continued, "Some of that stuff about the limited company sounds a bit dodgy but it doesn't sound like he would push Ted off a ladder."

"Better get you back to work," said Susan, "And thank you for acting as out bodyguard."

After dropping Mike off, Susan went round to Michelle and Colin's to explain why the phone call had ended so abruptly.

"I think we need a final case conference," she said. "How about tomorrow morning?"

o-O-o

Friday 2nd June

It was a gloriously sunny morning as the quartet gathered in Colin and Michelle's back garden.

Colin had dug out an old flip chart and easel which he'd been storing for a neighbour but when they'd moved, they'd told him to keep it. Michelle thought, 'more junk' but Colin stashed it at the back of his garage in his 'may come in handy one day' pile.

Susan held court.

"Well folks, I think that may be that. All our suspicions have been proven quite wrong unless those we've spoken to were fibbing."

"I agree," said Adrian. "Not a psychopath among them."

"The only person we've been unable to meet is my uncle's former business partner, Peter or Pete Wyatt", Susan continued. "He seems to have vanished into thin air. That being the case, I'd like to concentrate on wrapping up my uncle's estate. In the meantime, I think we'd be better just shelve all thoughts of an investigation and get on with our lives."

"Reluctantly, I think you're right," piped up Adrian. "Pity, I was quite enjoying being a private investigator."

"We could put a notice in the local paper," suggested Colin, "asking Pete Wyatt to contact us."

"I'd rather not," said Susan. "Anyway, if he's no longer living round here, or no longer living, full stop, it would be a wasted expense and effort. More tea anyone?"

"Fair enough", said Colin, and then dragging another ancient gag from his memory bank asked, "What do you call a man with garden compost all over his head?"

"Peat", said the other three in unison.

o-O-o

Saturday 3rd June

By now, Adrian's Saturday morning routine was falling into a pattern. He and Susan would share lifts to the park. Susan would go off on some crazy warm up leaving Adrian to perform some pseudo stretches, continuing his attempts to look like he knew what he was doing.

Keith was the tail walker again this week.

“Hi, Ades, how’s it going?”

Adrian opened his mouth to correct Keith but decided to let it go by simply replying, “Great, thanks, Keith.”

“I spotted you got a PB last week.”

“Yes, a few minutes quicker.”

As they set off, Adrian walked with Keith. “Last time we did this, you told me that you used to be a personnel manager.”

“Yes, that’s right, that is before they went all American and changed my job title to Human Resources Manager. I hated that. It made the staff sound like commodities.”

“So, here’s a scenario. Two partners trading in a successful small business. One decides to simply walk out after an argument, never to be seen again. Any recourse of any sort?”

“Unlikely, unless the partner who walked out was an employee of the other partner. If so, he could claim unfair dismissal on the grounds of bullying or discrimination."

"What about his half of the company's assets?"

"If he walked out without going through a formal dissolution of partnership, then he's had it, I'm afraid. He should have taken legal advice."

"Right. Thanks", said Adrian.

Keith looked down at Adrian's shoes. "If you don't mind a little piece of advice, if you're going to be doing parkruns regularly, I'd suggest you invest in a decent pair of training shoes."

"What would you recommend," asked Adrian.

"I'd suggest a visit to the running shop in Northwich. That's not too far away. It's called 'Sports and Running'. The young lass there is very helpful. She'll sort you out with something comfortable and not too expensive. And once you have a decent pair of shoes, why don't you try walking the first two laps and then when you reach the downhill bit on lap three, have a bit of a jog?"

"Great advice, thanks," said Adrian, before power walking off.

Adrian completed the parkrun in 49 minutes and 42 seconds, another small improvement.

On the way home, Adrian asked Susan if she had a spare hour or so to help him choose some suitable trainers. He wanted to continue with the parkrun and wished to take Keith's advice by visiting the running shop he'd described.

"I'm free on Monday morning," she said.

o-O-o

Monday 5th June

"Dring, dring" went the shop bell as Susan and Adrian walked in. The female shop assistant (who later turned out to be the proprietor) was serving a man who was asking if she stocked swimming trunks. She showed him a couple of pairs and he asked to try them on. The proprietor showed him to a small curtained-off corner of the shop.

"Hi, Emily," said Adrian, (as a good Private Detective, he had already read her name badge). "I am after a pair of training shoes suitable for walking. I've started doing the Saturday parkrun and need something more comfortable that these brogues."

Adrian was shown four pairs which he started to try on, a pair at a time.

As he was about to try on the second pair, the 'swimming trunks' man emerged from the curtained off changing area dressed only in a pair of speedos.

Susan and Adrian exchanged glances.

"What do you think? Do they fit OK?" he asked Emily.

"They look fine to me," she replied.

“What about round my bottom?” he asked, turning around and adopting a ‘Charles Atlas’ body builder stance. “Not too tight?”

“They’re just right,” said a slightly embarrassed Emily.

“OK, I’ll have them.”

After he had dressed and paid for his swimming trunks, he left.

Susan commented, “That was a bit out of order, wasn’t it? We were looking out for you in case that weirdo tried anything on.”

“That sort of thing happens very rarely,” said Emily. “It’s mostly serious runners who come here. But thanks. Anyway, I have a panic button which goes through to a monitoring company. They are linked to the police. If anything serious were to happen, I just press the footswitch behind the counter.”

“Have you ever stood on it by accident?” asked Adrian.

"Funnily enough, I did once. Within minutes a police car and two constables arrived, but they were OK about it."

"What do police officers put in their sandwiches?" asked Susan. "Truncheon meat!"

(Adrian shot her a surprised look).

The gag totally fell flat for three reasons – a) Susan's timing was terrible – she left no pause between the question and the punchline, b) it wasn't the least bit funny, and c) nobody under the age of 45 has ever heard of luncheon meat.

Meanwhile, Adrian was finding each of the four pairs of training shoes to be very similar, and all with a decent level of comfort. In the end he selected a pair based on colour and price – not too flashy and within his budget.

"Have a go on the treadmill," suggested Emily.

Emily started the machine at a four miles-per-hour pace and Adrian walked briskly. He mentally recalled the video of Peter Kay singing, 'Is this the way to Amarillo' and hoped he wouldn't do a Ronnie Corbett.

Adrian nodded approval before paying for the trainers. However, before leaving the shop, he whipped out the A4 sheet of paper with the image of the muddy footprint which he'd photographed from the side of Ted's ladder. Susan was taken aback as she had assumed the case was closed and besides, she'd forgotten all about Adrian's suspicions.

"Are you able to help us, Emily? Are you able to identify the type of training shoe from this image of the sole?"

Emily looked at it carefully. "It looks like it could be a fell shoe but honestly, it could be any one of a number of similar brands. It's possibly a Mudclaw." She went to her display and pulled down a box. Opening it, she compared Adrian's image with the sole of the shoe.

“Hmmm, possibly”. she said, “We sell a few of these to the Welsh fell runners who live just across the border.”

“How many would you say you sold in say the last three months?”

“Not that many. It’s the wrong time of year - possibly three or four pairs at most.”

“So, it would be fairly easy to draw up a list of purchasers?” ventured Susan.

“Blimey,” thought Adrian, “This girl’s good, sounding more and more like a private detective.”

“Two problems,” said Emily. “The first is customer confidentiality – I wouldn’t share customer information. And the second is the picture of the sole. That shoe has been around the block a few times. It is very worn. I doubt if it would be used for running, at least not recently.”

“OK, thanks,” said Susan.

As they were leaving the shop, Adrain spotted a dustbin-sized plastic bin in one corner. It was half full of assorted training shoes. It had sign taped to its front. The sign read, '*Trainers for the homeless - donate your unwanted shoes here*'.

"'Allo, 'Allo, 'Allo," said Adrian in a pantomime policeman's voice. "What have we 'ere?"

Susan thought this was really taking the private detective thing to extremes.

"Oh, that. That's our donation tub," volunteered Emily. "We collect used training shoes and pass them on to the James Wilson Mission where they, in turn, pass stuff on to the homeless. They can't get enough training shoes. They're very popular with the clients. We send old race tee shirts too. It's funny seeing people who've clearly never run in their lives, sitting in the Market Square wearing shirts with 'I ran the Manchester Marathon' and the like, emblazoned on the front".

"Hmm, that's coincidental. I'm off to the James Wilson Mission soon with a pile of my deceased uncle's clothes," said Susan.

o-O-o

Tuesday 6th June

Despite Michelle's phone call to Susan being abruptly interrupted by the mugger, Susan had subsequently been able to confirm to Michelle that Tuesday would be convenient for them to drop the bags of clothes off at the Mission.

When they arrived, they managed to squeeze the car into a tiny car park at the front of what had once been a small chapel. Outside there was a queue of about a dozen men.

Susan was first out of the car and said to the man nearest to the door, "Are you all waiting for the mission to open?"

"No, it is open", said the man, "but today is food bank day. We're called in one at a time to choose what we need, otherwise it would be a free for all. Just ring the bell and Dennis should be out to see you."

By now, Michelle had unloaded five bin liners of clothes and brought them to the door.

“Any coats in there?” the man at the front of the queue asked, “I need a warm coat for when I sleep out.”

“Sorry, no coats,” said Michelle.

“We could try to find one for you,” added Susan. “Will you be here next week?”

“I’m here tomorrow,” he said, “It’s breakfast club on a Wednesday. I’m Jim by the way.”

“Can’t promise anything, Jim, but you never know.”

Susan didn’t need to press the bell as Dennis opened the door to let one client out before ushering Jim in.

“Dennis?” asked Michelle. He nodded. “We spoke on the phone. I’m Michelle Wilkinson. We’ve brought the clothes we spoke about.”

“Come in,” said Dennis, grabbing three of the bags before bolting the door after them.

Dennis took Michelle and Susan (plus a bag each) through to a room with a faded nameplate on the door – ‘Vestry’.

“I’ll leave you with Mary,” said Dennis as he scuttled back to manage the food distribution in the main room.

“Quite an operation,” said Susan.

“Well, we try to make a bit of a difference”, said Mary. “It all started several years ago as a soup kitchen for people living on the streets. These days we provide a breakfast club on a Monday, Wednesday and Friday. As you can see, Tuesday is foodbank day, and Friday is clothes distribution day. We’ve found from experience that it works better if we split the different activities across the week.”

“Why are there mainly men?” asked Michelle.

"Just the way it has developed. I don't know the answer but the word on the street is that we cater for men."

"Where do they all come from?" asked Susan.

"It varies. Some are homeless and do live on the streets. Some pop over from the Christian hostel up the road. Others are totally broke. We don't ask any questions. Generally, we find they are all in need be it food or clothing. We rely on donations – food from the supermarkets and clothes from the general public. We rarely have any trouble. If anyone tries anything on, the clients themselves sort them out. They are very loyal to the mission."

"Are you all volunteers?"

"Yes, all volunteers."

"Marvellous," said Susan before adding, "We've got these clothes for you. They used to belong to my uncle. All in decent condition. I hope you can make use of them."

"Yes, of course," said Mary, "Thank you."

"Driving back to the close, Susan said, "Do you think my uncle's donkey jacket would be of any use to Jim? I'm thinking of popping back tomorrow."

"Can't do tomorrow, Sue, but maybe Adrian will be at a loose end, now he's hung up his deerstalker and magnifying glass."

o-O-o

Wednesday 7th June

Today was Adrian's birthday.

He wasn't expecting any cards, and it was too soon for Paul the postman.

At 09.30 Susan rang Adrian's bell. She was carrying Ted's donkey jacket which she'd retrieved from the garage. "Ready to go? Did you remember?"

"Yes, and yes," Adrian replied," I'll just pop my trainers on". Adrian liked wearing his new trainers.

Not only did this help to break them in, but he thought they made him look younger and cooler.

When they arrived at the mission, there was no queue outside, but they rang the bell anyway.

Dennis answered.

"Hi Dennis," announced Susan, "I'm Susan. I was here yesterday with a different friend. We brought a few bin liners of clothes. Mary took them from us."

"Ah, yes," said Dennis, slowly as his brain caught up with what Susan was saying, I remember. How can I help you today?"

From the main room they could hear a hubbub of conversation and the clatter of knives and forks on plates.

"Breakfast club today," said Dennis, before Susan passed over the coat, saying, "This is for Jim. He was after a coat when we called yesterday."

"Jim's not here. He's already been in, but I'll see he gets it. Now, I'm sorry but I need to get back to grilling more sausages."

Before he could close the door, one of the clients squeezed past him to leave.

"Bye, Pete," shouted Dennis.

Susan and Adrian shot each other glances. It would be a farfetched coincidence, but Adrian asked Dennis anyway, "Was that man by any chance, Peter Wyatt?"

"I'm sorry," smiled Dennis, "I'm sure you'll understand. The mission must retain total confidentiality. We are not able to give out any personal information."

"We understand," said Adrian before Dennis slowly closed the door.

When they turned round, there was no sign of 'Pete'. There were four streets leading away from the mission and he could have taken any one of them.

"It would be a very, very, longshot," suggested Adrian. "Maybe we should forget all about it."

"Nah!" said Susan. "It's worth following up, even though the odds are against us. Did you notice what he had on his feet – training shoes!"

"Nope, I didn't notice his shoes," said Adrian. "If you are really intent on following up on this, how about we do a bit of undercover surveillance at the next breakfast club?"

"Mary said there was one on Friday. How about we pop back then?"

"I hope we'll recognise him," suggested Adrian.

"We will if he's wearing the same clothes – light brown fleece jacket, cream trousers and those red training shoes."

"You're very observant," remarked Adrian, "Private Investigator material."

"Or simply a woman's eye for these things."

o-O-o

When the pair drove back into the close, they saw Michelle and Colin, walking towards Adrian's house with what looked like a tray, covered with a tea towel.

"Just popped across to wish you a Happy Birthday," said Michelle giving Adrian a quick peck on the cheek.

"Happy Birthday, old man," said Colin giving Adrian a card. "I'll pass on giving you a kiss, though."

"How did you get on at the mission?" asked Michelle.

"Funny you should ask. We think there's a slim chance we may have found Peter Wyatt," said Susan smugly.

They recounted what had happened, together with the stake out plan for Friday, before settling down to coffee and birthday cake, or in Susan's case, a fruit tea and no cake.

"On a more promising note," said Colin, "I've been going through Ted's files. I know you rang all the banks, Susan, but I discovered a website called,'mylostaccount.org.uk' – it's a free search service. I put in your uncle's details. After a day or two, they came back to me with a list, all of which you know about except for one. Have you heard of the Danske Bank. Neither had I. It's a Danish bank with a branch in Belfast. I didn't go any further until I spoke to you, Susan. I think you should contact them yourself to establish if there was any money in this account or whether if it is simply one of those dormant accounts with nothing in it."

"Interesting," said Susan. "I'm sure that the bookkeeper, what was her name, Tracy somebody, said that towards the end, my uncle made a couple of business trips to Ireland."

"Hang on," said Adrian, so have we reopened the case?"

"Sounds like it" replied Susan. "I'd like to speak to the bank first, though."

o-O-o

Thursday 8th June

Susan found the bank's details on the internet and telephoned the Customer Service phone number.

It was just after nine, so surely there would be someone to answer.

To her surprise, a young man's voice answered almost straight away. He had a delightful Irish brogue and said his name was Liam.

As she suspected, Susan was denied any access to her uncle's account. Liam wouldn't confirm or deny whether there was an account in her uncle's name. What he did say was he'd made a file note that Susan had telephoned to report the death. He'd also asked if Susan could forward a certified copy of the Death Certificate, in the event of the bank locating an account in the name of Edward Watt. Thereafter, if an account was located, the bank would need authority to let Susan access the details, either an original Probate or Letters of Administration.

Susan said she was awaiting the latter, as there was no will, and could send it if it was required.

o-O-o

Friday 9th June

Today was the day for operation "Stakeout".

Both Susan and Adrian were excited about either finding Peter Wyatt or else eliminating the mission's "Pete" from their enquiries.

They'd agreed to arrive outside the mission for nine o'clock. Adrian drove as the BMW might attract attention. Parking was a bit tricky. "Not like you see on TV, where there is a space conveniently waiting," thought Adrian.

He drove around the block in the hope that there would be a vacant space with a good sightline of the mission doorway, but it was no good. He drove round to the 'pay and display' near the

Market Square and was infuriated to find the machine no longer accepted cash.

"Don't worry," said Susan, "I have my card with me."

It seemed like you needed an IT degree to be able to fathom out which button to press and in what order. A lady, who was next in the machine queue, gave some helpful advice and soon a white ticket appeared.

The pair of Private Investigators walked back towards the mission. Susan spied a bench next to the bus stop about 25 yards away. They sat down and waited.

The mission seemed to be already open as mainly men either left or entered the building.

"Can you remember what time this Pete guy left on Wednesday," asked Adrian.

"I think it was about quarter to ten."

Susan was right. Almost exactly at 9.45, the same guy exited, wearing the same light brown fleece jacket, cream trousers and significantly wearing training shoes.

"OK, let's follow him," said Susan, "But don't make it obvious."

It was fairly easy to keep up with their quarry and he didn't look back. His route took him through the market square car park where Adrian noticed a traffic warden checking tickets on windscreens. He hoped he'd pressed the correct buttons. It was a £50 fine if he hadn't.

'Pete' crossed the small park and walked over the town centre ring road using a footbridge. This led to what had once been a posh part of town with large merchant houses, long since converted into residences of multiple occupation. By the time he caught up with Susan, Adrian found her leaning against a wall. He was puffing when he joined her.

"Did you lose him?" Adrian wheezed.

"Nope, He went in that large building over there. There's a nameplate on the gatepost – Gethsemane House. Seems like it's some sort of hostel. I noted the name down on my phone's notepad."

"Blimey. Didn't know you could do that. I'm a paper and pencil man myself." said Adrian. "Let's go back to the car and have a bit of a think about our next move."

Susan bowed to Adrian's judgement.

Once in the car, Susan suggested researching the hostel online. If there was a warden or hostel manager listed, they could ask for an interview.

"But how do we establish if 'Pete' is our Peter?" asked Adrian.

"Maybe see if we can take a photograph and then show it to one of the former employees?" answered Susan.

"Invasion of privacy," said Adrian. "Maybe one of the former staff would come with us on our next stake out."

"Mm. Let's go home and discuss it with the others."

After returning home and pleased that Colin was not prostrate on his front path again, Adrian invited his neighbours over for a mug of coffee and what remained of his birthday cake.

It was easy to fill them in with the brief sequence of events.

"I've got a great idea," suggested Colin. "Why don't I call there with a parcel for Mr. Peter Wyatt and see if he appears. If the warden says there is nobody by that name here, then we can eliminate him."

"Brilliant" said Susan. "When do you want to do this?"

"What about foodbank day, Tuesday?" offered Michelle.

"Great," said Colin, "I'll prepare my parcel and my uniform."

o-O-o

Saturday 10th June

Going to the parkrun was now feeling like a normal Saturday morning routine for Adrian. It meant he had a purpose for not lying in bed for too long. He enjoyed the atmosphere and had started to recognise the regulars who walked at his sort of pace. Susan didn't seem to mind finishing her race before coming back to look for him.

Once home, his endorphins were pinging, and he felt great. It was still just after ten, so after a quick shower and a mug of coffee, he could spend the rest of the morning reading his newspaper, guilt free.

o-O-o

Tuesday 13th June

"How do I look?" asked Colin.

"I just love a man in uniform," replied Michelle, a little sarcastically.

Colin had dug out his smart blue trousers and a matching blue polo shirt. He'd polished his 'funeral/wedding shoes'. In a drawer, he'd located an old ID badge which he'd been given at one of those boring accountants conferences. He changed the label insert by making a badge which said, 'CW Deliveries and Logistics'.

For his parcel, Colin had raided the sideboard where he'd found a large, unopened, tin of shortbread, a raffle prize which was very close to its 'consume by' date. He'd placed this in an Amazon delivery box which he'd retrieved from the corner of his study, and he'd used some posh brown paper to wrap it up convincingly. He added an official-type address label addressed to Mr. Peter Wyatt, c/o Gethsemane House.

Judging that Peter would be back at the hostel for about 10.00, Colin left the house soon afterwards.

Susan had found the name of the hostel manager, The Rev. Barnabus Pugh.

Colin parked a few doors away from Gethsemane House and marched purposefully to the front door. He rang the intercom.

"Reception. How can we help?"

"Parcel delivery," said Colin.

The intercom gave a buzzing sound and the door clicked open. Colin entered to find a reception desk in the hallway just in front of an imposing wooden staircase. Behind it sat a lady in a grey cardigan. She had a kindly looking face and smiled as Colin approached. "Good morning," she said.

"Morning," said Colin trying to sound like what he perceived to be delivery man speak. "Parcel for one of your residents, Mr. Peter Wyatt."

"Oh, I don't believe he's in at the moment. Would you like to leave it here?"

"Sorry, love, needs a signature. I'll try to pop back later."

With that, Colin told the lady to 'Have a good day' before making for the front door. He picked up a leaflet about the hostel, found his car and made his way home.

The others were gathered in Susan's kitchen eagerly awaiting his return.

"How did it go?" asked Adrian.

"Good news. I managed to get into reception and after I'd said I had a parcel for Mr. Peter Wyatt, I was told he wasn't in. She didn't say there was nobody by that name living there."

"What sort of a place is it?" asked Susan.

"According to their leaflet, the hostel is run by a consortium of several local churches. The head honcho is The Rev Barnabus Pugh. It's open to anyone who has fallen on hard times but there is a strict 'no alcohol, substance, or drugs', policy. Apparently, clients book in for an initial six months, during which the people there assist with welfare benefit applications and job hunting. It says that after six months, clients are expected to move on but the hostel staff try to keep in touch with them through telephone chats."

Sounds like we're getting pretty close," said Susan. "What should our next step be?"

"Definitely kettle on and let's crack open this shortbread," suggested Colin.

As they took their first sips of coffee, or in Susan's case, lemon tea, Susan said she had something to say.

"The Letters of Administration document arrived in this morning's post. It confirms that as next of kin, I am now able to sort out my uncle's estate. So, I'll need some time out to contact his banks and building societies and have all his accounts transferred into my name.

I'm going to take a bit of a break in a couple of days' time, maybe three or four weeks. I need to fly over to Belfast – business rather than pleasure.

Oh, and the big, big, news of the day is that I've decided to rent out my flat in Dartford and move north.

I need to go down there to sort out the rental arrangements with a managing agent."

After a period of stunned silence, Michelle was first to speak.

"Will you be moving into Ted's house?"

"My plan is this," said Susan. "Once his house is transferred into my name, I will own two properties, which is ridiculous. So, I'm going to put my uncle Ted's house on the market and use the proceeds to buy a small flat in town. I don't fancy looking after a garden and if I am near the town centre, I can flog the beamer and travel around on my bike."

"What about all your friends in Dartford?" asked Michelle.

“Yes, bit of a tough call, but you know, the pace and quality of life is so much better up here. People are more friendly too. I’ll still keep in touch with them. Anyway, it’s only two hours from Chester to Euston if I want to take a train to visit them.”

“What about your job?” asked Adrian.

“That’s going too. Bye, bye, rat race. I would be more than happy with a simple part time job with no pressure. Maybe a delivery driver running round in a small van taking car parts to garages.”

“Income?” asked Colin.

“From the proceeds of the property sale, I will pay cash for the new flat. If I get rid of the car, the rental income from the flat will mean I’ll be able to cope with my outgoings. Just food, gas, electricity, water, and Council Tax. I’m not a party animal and I don’t smoke or drink.”

“Blimey,” said Adrian, “You’ve really thought this through.”

"When do you think you'll be back, to resume the case?" asked Michelle.

"Probably in about three weeks. In the meantime, I'm guessing Peter Wyatt isn't going anywhere."

"More shortbread, anyone?" asked Colin.

o-O-o

The next three weeks

Adrian received a surprise phone call from his daughter, Liz, who lived with her family on Skye. They'd booked a short family break at the Peebles Hydro Hotel, about 20 miles south of Edinburgh. Liz wondered if Adrian would like to join them as it had been a while since he'd had a holiday. Adrian jumped at the chance. He managed to secure a single room and set about packing walking, swimming and even running kit for his break.

Colin said he'd keep an eye on the house while he was away.

Adrian's journey north was trouble free. He arrived at the hotel just as the check-in was opening. He was very pleased with his room and immediately felt positive and relaxed.

It was good to see his two grandchildren and to catch up with Liz and her husband. The swimming pool was good fun, especially tossing the children off the floating mats. When he announced that he'd be doing the Saturday parkrun, Liz was surprised. She was unaware that her dad had taken up running.

On the day, Adrian made his way to the park which was about a mile away. There didn't seem to be many runners there at all.

"It doesn't start until nine-thirty," said a marshall. "You must be an English tourist. They all turn up just before nine, not realising that all Scottish parkruns start later to avoid the dark winter mornings."

Adrian hung around and went through his stretches. Slowly more people appeared until it was time for the first timers briefing. After the first couple of sentences Adrian had lost the plot. The course seemed to go round and round and back and forth along several paths. He knew he wouldn't be leading, so assured himself that he'd simply follow the person in front.

On the word, "Go", Adrian managed a jogging pace. The start was downhill, and he was pleased to know there were people behind him. The course was indeed in and out. It was a small park, so the course had many loops to accommodate the 5k distance. At one point it went alongside the River Tweed before a cruel climb to the uppermost part of the course. This appeared three times during the race and by the third time, Adrian was struggling.

He wasn't as quick as his local parkrun, which was flatter. He felt tired but satisfied when he finally crossed the line.

"Well," he thought, "That's 'P' crossed off my A-Z of parkruns. Just twenty-four more to go."

After a shower and a cup of coffee, Adrian told Liz about the excellent children's play area he'd seen while jogging around the park. That afternoon, they packed a picnic and spent several hours there, catching up while the children paddled in the Tweed. Adrian told Liz about Ted's so-called accident and how he and Ted's niece were playing private detectives.

"You want to watch it," warned Liz. "Seriously. You don't know what Ted was into. He may have been involved with those smackheads from the Dale Farm Estate. He may have been money laundering, drug dealing, or he may even have owed someone money. If you dig too deeply, it could be you next."

Adrian hadn't thought about a darker side to Ted. Maybe he should leave well alone and opt for an easy life.

After four nights it was time for Adrian to return to Cheshire, suitably refreshed.

But once home, without Susan around, there wasn't anything to do on the case.

"Just as well," thought Adrian, remembering his daughter's stern words of warning.

Adrian attended the next two local parkruns and though he could detect an almost weekly improvement in his fitness, he missed the pre- and post-race banter with Susan. Acacia Close seemed quieter too. No Whirling Dervish regularly sprinting up the close after a quick 8-mile run.

Adrian busied himself with his, and Susan's, gardens while Colin and Michelle had a weekend away in North Wales.

o-O-o

Sunday 3rd July

On his return, Colin had arranged another of his barbeques on the grass patch in the centre of the close. Although it was a day too early, his theme was, 'American Independence Day'. He'd dressed up in a checked shirt and cowboy hat and had erected some stars and stripes bunting. His sound system was blasting out his 'Country and Western greatest hits' CD to the irritation of

Adrian who couldn't stand all that wailing about wrecked trains and wrecked relationships.

As the neighbours gathered for their lunchtime burgers, Susan's BMW pulled in to the close. A cheer went up.

"Oooh, food," she shouted, "Any veggie sausages?"

"No, sorry," said Colin, "but there's loads of salad."

After Susan had parked up, taken her suitcase into the house, and freshened up, she joined the neighbours. She'd dug out a checked blouse which she'd knotted across her middle, some white jeans and some long brown boots.

"Yee-Har," she shouted, before adding quietly to Adrian, "I'll update the team tomorrow. I'm conscious that the people from the other houses were not party to the recent investigations."

"Why was the burger embarrassed?" asked Colin.

Everyone carried on talking.

"Because it saw the salad dressing," he replied to a non-listening audience.

o-O-o

Monday 4th July

Colin and Michelle made their way across to Adrian's house for their prearranged ten o'clock conference. Colin was carrying the last of the shortbread.

Once settled, Susan led off.

"First off, I've been down to Dartford and I've put my flat on the rental market. The estate agent thinks it will go very quickly, so watch this space. I'll put next door on the market too once I've secured a property in town."

"Next." (The others knew by now not to interrupt once Susan was in full flow).

"My trip to Belfast was great. I stayed two nights in a Premier Inn and as well as visiting the Titanic exhibition, I went to see the people in the Danske Bank. I'd already made an appointment to register my name as administrator of my uncle Ted's estate. I was astonished, gobsmacked, and every other adjective you can think of, to discover that my uncle had a very large balance. There's well over half a million! I couldn't believe it, especially when I thought of all those former members of his staff who are now signing on for unemployment benefit. Anyway, the account is now in my name, and I just need a bit of time to consider what to do with the money."

Colin sat back in the chair with an audible exhalation of air whistling through his teeth.

"Apart from all that," continued Susan, "I'd like to reopen the case and hopefully put everything to bed once and for all."

"Blimey," said Adrian, "Sounds like your uncle was creaming off the company profits for some considerable time. What a cad." Adrian said nothing about Liz's warning about drug dealers and score settling. Susan's enthusiasm had excited him and he felt ready to poke around some more, even if this was a high-risk strategy.

After about an hour of catch-up chit-chat, Susan said that she'd now like to plan the conclusion of the case.

"I think all that's outstanding is to have a chat with Pete or Peter Wyatt, now that we've discovered where he lives," she continued. "Just need a strategy. Do we approach as private investigators or me, as Uncle Ted's niece?"

"I'd say you as the niece and me as a business support person," said Adrian. "That way we can start gently by talking about the collapse of the business without scaring him off. We'd need to choose a time and place, though."

"We know his movements, roughly," said Colin. "You could intercept him after the breakfast club and maybe take him to the park."

"Yes, I'd go with that", said Susan. "Adrian?"

"Yes, good idea. How about the next breakfast club on Wednesday?"

o-O-o

Wednesday 6th July

Susan and Adrian waited on the bus stop bench outside the mission, about 50 yards away, and watched all the comings and goings. As anticipated, at 09.45, Peter exited, wearing the same clothes as previously.

Without saying anything, Susan and Adrian followed at a safe distance behind him. After crossing the ring road bridge, they sped up, and by the time he'd reached the front door of Gethsemane hostel, Susan called out, "Peter Wyatt?"

Peter span round in surprise, gazing at their two faces and trying to work out who they were.

"It's alright," said Susan. "I am a relative of the late Ted Watt and I was wondering if we could have a bit of a chat."

Peter looked like he didn't know how to answer.

"How about we grab some takeaway coffees from the park café and find a bench in the sunshine?" suggested Susan.

Peter nodded. He hadn't asked who Adrian was and Adrian didn't feel the urge to provide any explanations at this stage.

Their walk to the coffee kiosk and park bench took about five minutes during which time there was little conversation.

Once settled, Susan began.

"Peter, did you know that Ted Watt is no longer with us? He died after falling off his ladder while he was cleaning out his gutters."

"I did hear something on the grapevine," he mumbled.

"I'm his next of kin. I travelled up from Kent a few weeks ago in order to sort out my uncle's affairs. I'd heard that you were his business partner once".

Peter stared into his coffee cup.

"I was really hoping you'd be able to tell me a little bit more about the business."

"Nightmare," said Peter.

"Yes, I've been hearing it wasn't a pleasant place to work and it was tragic for the staff when it went into compulsory liquidation This is my friend, Adrian. He's a business adviser. Maybe it would be best if he took you through what happened."

"I'd rather not revisit the ghosts of the past," said Peter.

"Maybe if I speak and you nod," suggested Adrian. "We've heard that you started the business off but after a while Ted joined as co-partner. It sounds like things went well to begin with, but later Ted turned into a bit of a controlling individual. I heard that the company expanded too fast and ran up a lot of debt. In my opinion, you got out at the right time."

"Did I?" said Peter despondently.

Susan chipped in, "Piecing together everything that happened, I have reached the conclusion that my uncle was not a very nice person. You can talk freely with us. It may help me to understand what went on."

Peter drained his coffee cup and took a deep breath. Speaking quietly and slowly he began to open up.

"Seems like you know the story already. I ended up walking out and leaving that rat to it. I probably made a mistake. I suffered from a nervous breakdown. Not easy when you live alone. The building society were the first to come after me. I tried rescheduling my mortgage payments but soon I was in arrears. They repossessed the house and I found myself sofa surfing for a while before that all finished. Downhill from there. It is so demoralising sleeping rough. My saviour was Barnabus. He was walking through the park one day and stopped for a chat. He suggested the hostel until I got back on my feet. Lovely people in there, so kind. I have to contribute a few bob each week towards my housekeeping but I don't think I'm any trouble. Any boozers get kicked out straight away and I'm not into drugs. The mission is good too. No questions asked. Free food and free clothing too. God, I've fallen a long way to end up like this. I was a personal trainer once and now look at me. Where will it all end?"

"How are you financing yourself?" asked Adrian in a paternal manner.

"I sign on for dole, or Universal Credit as it's known these days. But I have a little job delivering leaflets. It's so low paid it doesn't affect my benefits, but it gets me out of the hostel and it means I have exercise and fresh air."

"Very important," said Susan.

Adrian glanced down at Peter's training shoes. He could just pick out the word, 'Mudclaws' on the side of one of them.

"Where do you do your leafleting?" asked Adrian.

“I’m a bit choosy,” said Peter. “I don’t touch the Dale Farm estate. Too much aggro. I prefer the better off houses.”

“Ever do pizza leaflets in Acacia Close?” asked Adrian.

Peter shot Adrian a glance which was somewhere between disbelief and fear. Without warning, he stood up and ran away. Susan chased him but not only did he have a head start but he reached the middle of the pedestrian bridge over the ring road first. He spun round and shouted to Susan, “Don’t you come any closer or I’ll jump!”

Adrian pulled out his phone as he tried his best to run. He speed-dialled Colin, as he went. Even though Colin answered after four rings, it felt like a lifetime.

“Peter’s gone berserk. He’s gonna jump off the by-pass bridge – the one in the park. Can you get down here ASAP?” Adrian shouted.

As Adrian reached the end of the bridge, Susan sped away into the trees on his left.

"No closer, or I <u>will</u> jump," shouted Peter.

"No, don't do anything silly," shouted Adrian. He'd never been in a situation like this before and had no clue as to the best thing to say or do.

Peter climbed on to the guard rail overlooking the southbound lane of the by-pass. "Stay there," he shouted.

They seemed to be locked in stares for ages, probably about three or four minutes while each wondered what to do next. "Where did Susan disappear to?" wondered Adrian, "and where was Colin – he's taking his time".

Suddenly two things happened simultaneously. Colin's car roared into the nearby car park. Colin and Michelle jumped out. This distracted Peter for a moment just as Susan appeared at the far end of the bridge. She'd sprinted the short distance to the next bridge over the bypass and doubled back on the other side. She ran quietly on her toes without Peter detecting her approach. She swiftly grabbed him from behind in a firm bear hug.

Adrian ran forward to assist. Between them, they managed to manhandle Peter off the bridge and into the park next to Colin and Michelle.

They heard the sound of a police siren approaching.

"Quick!" said Susan to Colin, put Peter's fleece on and stand in the middle of that bridge".

"And?"

"Busk it," shouted Adrian as he, Susan and Michelle took Peter to Colin's car.

A few seconds after Colin took up position on the bridge, he saw a police car drive up to the far end. Two officers jumped out and walked briskly towards him.

"Don't move," said the first and, conversely, "Come away from the railing," said the second.

The first officer drew a taser. "That's a bit OTT," thought Colin, "In the TV programmes they always talk the person down calmly."

"Can I help you?" said Colin in a disarming way.

"Don't jump!" shouted the first officer.

"Jump?" asked Colin incredulously, "Why would I want to jump?"

"A passing motorist reported a jumper on the bridge," said the second officer.

"No jumpers, here," said Colin, "unless you are referring to this one I'm wearing."

"So, what are you doing on the bridge?"

"I'm helping a mate out."

"Doing what?"

"Lorry spotting."

"Lorry spotting?"

"Yup. My mate's heavily into spotting Eddie Stobart trucks. There's a brand-new Volvo tractor unit and trailer due this morning just about now. It's coming down from the Runcorn depot. My mate can't make it so he asked me to snap it on my phone."

For good effect, Colin looked down on a piece of paper he was holding. "Registration ES23THS," he said.

The first police officer pulled out his radio. "Sierra Tango to control, over."

"Sierra Tango receiving," cackled the radio.

"All units heading for the Park Bridge incident to stand down. False alarm. Over."

"Must have missed that truck," said Colin. "Anyway, it's nearly lunchtime, need to grab a sandwich."

"Same here," said the second officer.

"Really?" said Colin, "What do Police Officers have in their sandwiches?"

"Brie and grapes for me," said the first, leaving Colin totally stuck for words.

"By the way," said the first copper, "Your mate's winding you up big style. Eddie Stobart went bust about three years ago!"

Colin simply turned, waved, and walked back to his car.

o-O-o

As he climbed into the driving seat, he gave Peter his fleece. Peter was sat in the middle of the back seat between Susan and Michelle. Adrian was sitting in the front passenger seat looking very red-faced. "Where to, guvnor?" Colin asked in a cockney cabbie type voice.

"Let's all go to my place," offered Adrian.

Back in the lounge, Adrian reverted to his tried and tested tea and biscuits routine. He soon appeared with a tray containing cups, saucers, plates, a sugar bowl, a teapot, serviettes, and a plate with Fox's Assorted biscuits on it.

But this time, in an attempt to relieve some of the tension, Adrian did say, "I'll be mother."

Once everyone had a drink, Susan stood up and said she wanted to outline how she saw things, "Without interruption, please."

She briefly went through how she'd first heard about her uncle's death and how she's gradually learned what an unpleasant and unscrupulous man he'd been, especially to his staff and his ex-business partner, Peter. She spoke about being the sole beneficiary of her uncle's estate and, with that in mind, how she'd spoken to several former employees to learn more about the business. She went on to describe Adrian's suspicions that her uncle's fall may not have been an accident. Then she paused.

"I did it", said a very quiet voice, then the voice repeated, "I did it," much louder.

It was Peter's voice.

Susan decided to let him continue.

"I've been suffering from terrible depression. It just built up more and more ever since I packed the job in a year or so ago. A few months back, when I was delivering my leaflets, I unexpectedly found myself here in this close. I realised it was Ted Watt's road as I'd been to his house a couple of times. When I came into the close, he was up a ladder clearing out his front gutters, but by the time I'd leafletted the other houses, he'd climbed down and had moved through to the back. I returned to Ted's house. As I slipped round the back, he didn't see me. He was up his ladder clearing out the rear gutters. On impulse. I gave the ladder a sharp kick and he started to go. Those plastic fascia boards are very slippy – he should have propped his ladder against the brickwork."

Peter paused and took a deep breath.

"I didn't mean to kill him. I just wanted to teach him a lesson. After I found out he was dead, I was sorry I'd done it. I was sick with worry and expected the police to come knocking any day but as time went on, even though I thought I'd got away with it, the enormous guilt led me in a downward spiral of melancholy. I'm pleased you've all taken the time to listen to my story. Already I feel a sense of relief."

After another pause, Peter sighed heavily and said, "I suppose you're going to turn me in now?"

"No!" said Susan sharply, "Nobody here is going to turn you in." She caught Adrian's eye as his face told a story of incredulity.

"This is the situation," said Susan. "Firstly, the coroner has declared the cause of death as accidental following a fall from height. That's what's recorded on my uncle's death certificate, and I see no reason to seek an amendment. Secondly, you were treated very badly, and so were many others – staff and suppliers. I suspect my uncle received what was coming to him, deservedly in my view. If it hadn't been you, his crazy antics on top of that ladder would have led to the same outcome. Finally, I think you have been through enough what with losing your job, your house and probably your self-respect. What would a prison sentence achieve? Several years of misery stuck in a two-man cell with a stranger for 23 hours a day, as well as all that slopping out. No, my friend, you can live the life of a free man."

Peter was completely lost for words.

"And that's not all," added Susan. "I'm going to make it my business to help you to get your life back again. The first thing I'm going to do is to reimburse the company's money which went walkabout. I have managed to recover a large sum of money which my uncle Ted took out of the firm and squirrelled away in a Belfast bank account. This belongs to you. If you still have your personal bank account, I will transfer the funds across. Even after tax, there will still be enough for you to buy a modest two-bedroomed house locally, and still have a decent sum left over to invest for a regular income. I have asked, Colin, here, who is a chartered accountant, to provide any help you may need in this regard."

Colin sat there open mouthed but thought it best to nod and say nothing.

Peter sat there shaking his head in disbelief.

"I've just got one more thing to add," said Susan. "Do you remember Mike Abbott, one of the Watt and Wyatt personal trainers?"

Peter nodded.

"You know he set up on his own and now employs Tracy?"

Peter tried to say, "Yes," but his throat was very dry.

"I had a chat with Mike recently. He's opening a new fitness gym in an empty shop in Northwich, soon. He's asked Tracy to manage it for him but that leaves a vacancy in his present fitness centre. He remembers you as being particularly good with clients and wondered if you'd be interested in a couple of days a week to start with. It would be on a trial period of three months just to make sure you are each happy with the arrangement. If a permanent contract comes out of that, then Mike is prepared to increase your hours providing the business continues to grow. How does that sound?"

By now Peter was sobbing quietly into his handkerchief. That set Michelle off too. Colin started to crack up and had to leave the room. Adrian was in total awe at Susan's reasoned speech.

"This is going to take a few weeks to sort out, Peter, so I'm afraid you'll be staying at the hostel for a bit longer. In the meantime, I'm going to use some of my uncle's money to make donations to both the mission and to Gethsemane House."

After a brief pause, Susan announced, "Right. That's that then. Peter, how do you fancy joining the four of us for a full-blown roast dinner at the Toby Carvery, and I'm paying?"

o-O-o

Postscript - What happened next?

The mugger on the canal towpath

On the day when Susan had her phone snatched, there were several other people on the canal towpath. A mature cyclist not only witnessed the bike being thrown into the canal, but his bike-mounted camera recorded it. When he returned home, he edited the clip to isolate the footage before sending it to Cheshire Police.

The Police sent a screenshot of the young man's face to the Chester Chronicle. The following week, a photograph was published with a "Do you recognise this person?" statement.

Several people named the young man and the Chronicle passed the details to Cheshire Police. He was charged with fly tipping. He received a two-year suspended sentence plus an order to complete 15 hours of community service for the Canal and Rivers Trust. He was also fined £150 to cover the Trust's costs in recovering the bike from the canal.

Neil Mowatt, Solicitor

A widow entrusted Neil Mowatt to manage her finances by selecting appropriate investments to maintain a regular income. He not only mismanaged the portfolio but defrauded her by transferring a large portion of her savings into his name. After members of her family raised suspicions, the fraud office became involved. He was arrested, charged and sentenced to 2 years in prison. He was also struck off the Law Society register.

PC Olivia Briers
Liv resigned from the police service to retrain as a social worker.

Ian Smart, accountant
Ian commenced studying for the final two parts of his professional accountancy examinations with a view to advancing his career.

DI Roberts
Shortly after his visit to Adrian's house, DI Roberts took sick leave for three months before retiring from the police service on the grounds of ill-heath. Shortly after that he died after suffering from a massive heart attack while climbing the stairs.

Mike and Tracy
Mike continued to do well with his gym. The business expanded when Tracy took over the

second gym in Northwich. Tracy is now doing what she always wanted to do and is very happy.

Peter Wyatt

Peter took up Mike's offer and soon was providing personal training advice and running fitness classes in Mike's premises. He made such good progress and brought in sufficient new business, that Mike offered him a full-time position. He left the hostel after using Susan's money to purchase a modest, but recently refurbished, two-bed semi-detached property near to Mike's premises. His depression has lifted the point of having almost disappeared.

Susan

Susan moved out of her uncle's house and put it up for sale. It sold quickly. She is now living in the town centre close to all amenities. She is a regular runner with the local running club and continues to participate in the parkrun every Saturday morning. Susan loves living in the north but occasionally visits her friends in Dartford. She never did find a vacancy for 'a delivery driver running round in a small van taking car parts to garages.' Instead, she volunteers for two days a week at the Women's Centre on the Dale Farm Estate where she provides practical help to women who have been affected by drugs, or by those around them who are drug users.

Colin and Michelle

Colin was the first neighbour to welcome the new tenants who moved into Ted's old house. They are a young couple with two children aged 5 and 7 – an appreciative audience for Colin's endless jokes. Michelle thinks the family has brought new life to the close which now looks a little less like a retirement village. Michelle continues with her voluntary work. Colin still organises the close barbeques and assists Peter with his investments. Unsurprisingly, Colin has commenced preparing a book of 'Jokes for 7-year olds' which he hopes to self-publish soon.

Adrian

Adrian benefitted immensely from his involvement in the investigation. It gave him a new focus, as does the parkrun. He never misses these days and last Saturday scored another personal best of 39 minutes, so he's clearly doing some actual running for most of the time. He feels fitter and he can tighten the belt on his trousers a couple more holes than previously.

Adrian and Susan

A week after that momentous Wednesday when Susan's summing up and kindness towards Peter brought 'The Acacia Close Mystery' to a conclusion, Adrian invited Susan out for a posh dinner. He mooted that there was a proposal in the offing.

Disappointingly, there was no romance in the air that evening. Adrian was still missing Pat, so any dalliance would have felt a bit like betrayal. As for Susan, after her hurtful experience all those years ago, Susan is a confirmed and very happy singleton.

No, Adrian's dinner invitation was to discuss a proposal far more exciting than romance - a new venture – Crawley and Watt – Private Investigators.

Printed in Great Britain
by Amazon